THE FOREST

LISA QUIGLEY

PMMP

Perpetual Motion Machine Publishing
Cibolo, Texas

The Forest
Copyright © 2021 Lisa Quigley

All Rights Reserved

ISBN: 978-1-943720-62-0

www.PerpetualPublishing.com

Cover Art by Matthew Revert

For Fallon, who made me a mother and taught me that mama love has teeth, and for Frances, who showed me I would let my body be cut open to keep my children safe.

PART ONE

TRANSGRESSION

Part One

Transfusion

CHAPTER ONE
PRESENT

CHARLIE IS SLEEPING like the dead. I take his pulse to make sure he's still alive, that I haven't inadvertently killed him. Protecting Jonas is my top priority, but I would much rather do so without slaughtering the man who, up until two days ago, I deeply loved.

There is a sharp stab in my groin, wild emotion manifested as physical pain.

Of course, I still love him. That's not something that just goes away.

But he has betrayed me in a way I could have never anticipated, and that's a wound that won't heal easily. Probably not ever.

The dark, abysmal depression sucks at me. If I allow myself to submerge, I may never find my way back out.

I won't think about Charlie. There isn't time to be heart sick.

I have changed into brown corduroy pants, a grey thermal shirt, and a green and brown flannel shirt. Over that, I wear my warm green jacket. Neutral colors. Forest colors. I want to blend in. To be camouflaged. It is early fall, yes, but the forest is still green with only the faintest whispers of yellow. It's been unseasonably warm this month—a small grace for which, at this moment, I feel unbearably grateful—but it still gets chilly at night, and this time of year, the weather can be unpredictable. I am wearing waterproof hiking boots, and warm wool socks. Charlie's knife is tucked into my back pocket.

It's for food, I tell myself. In an emergency, I can kill a rabbit or squirrel. The thought makes me squeamish, but I will do what I need to be nourished. To stay alive for my son, I can do it. I could do anything for him.

I already am.

I go into the kitchen and chug a glass of water. "Better to carry water in your body than on it," Charlie told me once, when he was sharing his wilderness survival skills. Always a forest explorer and adventurer in my own right, I never really had to worry about danger in Edgewood's borders. I am grateful for his insights, now, and I hope they serve me well.

Next, I collect Jonas from his perch on my bedroom floor. He, too, is dressed in warm layers, and his body is soft and drooping. He is tired. My stomach churns. Adjusting to the lack of sleep in those early newborn days had been the most grueling part of early parenthood. Neither Charlie nor I had ever experienced anything like it. But with consistency (and, at times, pure desperation) we'd finally gotten him into a routine that allowed us all some blissful rest.

The amount he sleeps now is a blessing compared to those early days and since finding a schedule and routine that works, I've been so careful to adhere to it. But I don't have a choice. I am hoping he will sleep the night strapped to my chest, while I walk for as long and as far as I can tonight. I only have a very small window to get ahead and I must make it count.

Soon, they'll realize that I'm gone.

I strap Jonas into the baby carrier, his belly pressed up against my own. He settles his left cheek against my breast and I give him a pacifier. Already his eyelids are drooping.

4

The Forest

Once I am wearing Jonas, I pull on a wool hat. Then I hoist the backpack over my shoulders. Even though I've only packed essentials, it's heavier than I would have liked. It will have to do.

Jonas' eyelashes, like downy feathers, rest on his cheek. I kiss the top of his head, which is protected by a warm cap.

"Let's go, baby boy," I whisper. "We're going on an adventure."

I was hoping the words would cheer me up, but they just make me feel worse. Resolve curdles and solidifies in my groin.

There is no changing my mind now.

I step onto the porch. It is already dark out, and the entrance to the wooded trail is about fifty feet away from our back door.

The trailhead seems to yawn, stretching open like a wide, black mouth.

My pulse quickens.

I rub the gentle curve of Jonas' spine instinctively.

I love the woods, but I have always held a healthy respect for the woods at night. The woods at night are not always a friendly place for humans.

I try not to think about what might be living in there, besides animals. What might be waiting for me just inside that inky blackness.

Stop it.

I blink and swallow.

These dark thoughts are not helping anyone. Least of all myself. My pulse throbs. I am afraid. There. I thought it, I've admitted it. Now it's time to let it go, to move past it.

It's time to enter the dark forest.

I reach for the large wooden walking stick we keep by the back door.

For support, I tell myself. *To help with my burden.*

And behind that thought, another: *To beat off anything that wishes to do us harm.*

And just as I descend the final step, a figure emerges from behind the house, blocking my path.

"I had a feeling you might try to leave."

It's my mother.

CHAPTER TWO
BEFORE THE FOREST

MY BABY IS DEAD.
The thought vibrated against my skull, loud and immediate.

I stabbed a piece of popcorn with my needle, focusing on the satisfying way it slid through to the other side. My hands shook.

My baby died while I was laughing.

I impaled another piece of popcorn, this time so violently I pricked my finger with the needle. A red pearl formed on my fingertip, and I lifted it to my mouth. Suck. Drew in a trembling breath.

These thoughts were terrible, and they were also lies.

Jonas was in the living room, strapped to my husband's chest in the canvas baby carrier. Relinquishing control, giving Charlie space to be a father—these were things I'd been working on. That it took so much focused effort was astonishing. Logically I knew the absurdity of the panic that surged in my chest when my son wasn't in my direct line of sight, or better, physically connected to me. *Knowing* didn't make my fear any less real. The intrusive thoughts were relentless. It was irrational to believe my baby wasn't safe. We were in Edgewood, after all.

Charlie's mother had been helping me work through it.

She was the only one I was not ashamed to tell. She had been on the brink of death when they arrived in Edgewood. Stage four cancer in her breasts, her lymph nodes, her ovaries—the specific kind of horrific that most people only read about on the news, but which Charlie's mother—and, by proxy, her family—had to live through. Being from outside of Edgewood, she understood what was happening to me. *Postpartum anxiety*. She told me, though, I had to trust Charlie's love for our son, his instincts as a father, despite my worry. Charlie had to find his own way into fatherhood.

She was right, of course.

Or so I had believed.

I was making strands of popcorn garlands with my siblings in preparation for the fall festival. Lengths of our assembled garland looped over the ends of the table and a giant bowl of popcorn that Blossom just refreshed was at the table's center. This moment was nostalgic, familiar, yet I felt myself as incongruous within it. Everything was the same as it had been my whole life. I was the one who had changed.

The music that is my whole family surrounded me, but all I felt was the gaping absence where Jonas should be.

My skin itched. Did Charlie know to make sure Jonas' nose wasn't blocked by the carrier? A vein in my neck throbbed. Would Charlie place his hand on Jonas' back to ensure it still rose and fell? I wiped damp hands on my jeans. What if Charlie wasn't vigilant? I pictured us releasing Jonas from the carrier to discover that he was cold and blue and *it was too late*. My teeth vibrated. My hands returned to the table. I stabbed another piece of popcorn.

But it wasn't popcorn. Jonas' skin was blue and when I reached for him, I forgot the needle. My hand slipped and it punctured my dead baby's eyeball. It oozed clear, thick liquid.

I gasped and dropped the needle.

My stomach hitched; my chest tightened. My pulse throbbed against my neck and I squeezed my eyes shut but it was too late. The images were burned into my memory, real as though they'd actually happened.

My insides churned with shame. Where were these images coming from? Why did every single mundane thing I did lead to perpetual scenarios of impending doom?

My baby could be dead and I'd have done nothing to stop it.

The thought that I'd have the audacity to sit there and laugh with Arrow and Blossom, *to enjoy myself*, while my baby slipped away from this world was unbearable.

I stabbed a piece of popcorn so fiercely it split in two.

The light smack of something soft hitting me in the center of my forehead startled me. I breathed in deeply to absorb the depth of the aromas of cinnamon and pumpkin and yeast mingling in my mother's warm kitchen to ground myself in the comfort of home.

"What did that popcorn ever do to you?" It was Blossom. Beneath her mirthful teasing was something more serious: concern.

I blushed. "Nothing. Overeager."

The offending object that hit my forehead was now on the table in front of me: a particularly plump piece of popcorn. I picked it up. Arrow sat across from me, his fire-brown eyes watching me with a mixture of mockery and something else, something more intense that disquieted me.

Blossom, sitting next to me at the table, playfully jabbed a finger into my side.

"Earth to Faye." Her face was round, her cheeks pink—possibly from the warmth of the kitchen and definitely from youth, but also from the half glass of wine that Mom allowed her to have. She's turning twenty-one later this year; she's six years younger than me and it is always hard for me to believe that the plump face of this gorgeous young woman belongs to my baby sister. I could still hear the way my mother wailed when Blossom made her entrance into this world.

The abyss was ever near, drawing me closer with a magnetic roar that filled up my ears with buzzing. It was hungry for me, feeding on me from the inside out. The only thing akin to relief was being skin to skin with Jonas, was seeing with my own eyes that he was breathing. Seeing him safe.

But this was Edgewood. *Of course* he was safe. We all were.

I squeezed the bare skin on Blossom's soft arm, just to stay grounded.

"Sorry," I said. "I'm just—" I searched for a good excuse, but I didn't have one.

"Some town steward you'll be." The spite in Arrow's voice alarmed me.

"*Arrow*," Blossom hissed. She squeezed my arm back.

"What? It's like we can't say anything to her anymore," Arrow said.

I winced, but he was right. My family had been treating me with kid gloves for months. They sensed that I was off but couldn't articulate why. And how could I blame them? It's not as though I'd volunteered information. How could I? Mental illness didn't happen in Edgewood, wasn't something anyone in our town had ever needed to support their loved ones in. They were out of practice. They'd never been *in* practice.

I barely understood it myself, had no idea what was happening to me until Charlie's mother recognized the signs. She had postpartum anxiety with both her children and had quietly mentored me through it, respecting my requests for privacy. I didn't want my family to suspect my brokenness.

Arrow had always resented me for being the oldest, as if that's something I could help. He's only two years younger than me, but in his view, he was born three years too late. He would never be town steward and it grated on him.

10

"But I'm the oldest *boy*," he used to tell my mother, which always earned him a sharp glare.

"You know that's not how it works," she would tell him sharply. "Gender has nothing to do with it. Faye is the firstborn."

Except it wasn't untrue, not entirely. I was not the firstborn child of this family: the true firstborn was no longer alive. The thought made me flinch and mentally I flicked it away, a bug that buzzes with the endless hunger of the roaring darkness.

I didn't know all the details, just that my sister Autumn died before I was born. It was a truth I avoided looking at too closely, scared of what it could imply. If nothing bad was permitted to happen in Edgewood, how could an infant have died. The roar became louder. I didn't want to think about babies dying.

As town stewards, it was my family's job to nurture this town, ensure things ran smoothly, protect it. Keep it a safe haven.

With the hand not holding the popcorn, I touched the beaded Rowan necklace around my neck. The gesture was a habit. The necklace had been crafted for my older sister when she was born and gifted to me after her death. It made me feel close to her; I'd worn it for so long that the weight of it around my neck was as much a part of me as a limb. A book in my dad's study claimed that the wood of the Rowan tree was a guard against evil spirits and wicked enchantments. We weren't in need of any such charms in Edgewood—its very existence was a guard against all manner of evils—but still, it was a totem in its own right. A familiar, soothing comfort. Something solid for my fingers to cling to when the first terrible question raged, followed—always—by the one that was quieter, and worse.

What happened to Autumn?

(*And can it happen to my son?*)

CHAPTER THREE
PRESENT

MY MOTHER'S FACE appears gaunt and menacing in the harsh glare of the back porchlight. She has more grey hairs than I remember, and they form a wiry and wild halo around her stern face.

"It pains me to do this," she says, stepping forward.

"Me, too," I reply.

I don't think, I just act.

The walking stick connects with the side of her head, and the crack is sickeningly loud. Hot saliva fills my mouth.

First my mother just looks stunned. Then her eyes become vacant. She crumples to the grass.

My heart throbs painfully.

Have I killed my own mother? Oh, god, what has happened to us? I feel like I'm dreaming. Like I've entered some bizarre alternate reality. The thought makes me dizzy and nauseous, and the dark abyss looms once again.

Snap out of it.

There will be time to think about all of this later, to question, to wonder, to ache.

Now is the time for action. I need to move.

I may have even less time than I had originally planned.

With some exertion—the weight of the backpack is

already pulling at me—I kneel to check my mother's pulse.

She is alive, at least, but doubt gnaws at me. With Charlie knocked out on the couch in the living room, this is the second unconscious body on my hands in one evening.

My mother may very well be concussed, but I can't allow myself to worry about that now. She made her choices. I've made mine.

"Faye!" A harsh whisper in the dark, and startled, I look up as yet another figure emerges from the shadows.

A swell of panic, but then my body softens. "Blossom."

Her eyes meet mine, then slide to the ground. She takes in our mother, collapsed to the earth next to me. "Is she—"

"No. I wouldn't kill her."

"Of course not," Blossom says quickly, rushing to us. She kneels at my mother's other side. "I just meant—"

"I had no choice. I didn't want to."

She looks up at me, gaze steady and even. "Faye, I'm sorry."

I nod, once, curtly, then shake my head. "You were trying to help."

"I should have listened."

"Yes. You should have. But we're here now, and I don't have much time."

"I just thought—I hoped—"

"Yeah. Me too."

"I'm here to help."

I gesture toward our mother on the ground. I grab her beneath both armpits and Blossom lifts from her ankles. Together, we carry her through the door of our enclosed back porch and place her on the little couch.

Once she's situated, I pause and place a hand to Jonas' back in the baby carrier. I am already breathing heavily from these exertions. I am woefully tired. I look at my mother, knocked out on the couch, a trickle of blood dripping down her temple. "This isn't right," I whisper.

Blossom grips my shoulders, leans forward to press her forehead against mine. Jonas squirms between us. "No, it isn't." Her breath is hot against my face. "Go. I'll watch her."

"Charlie . . ."

The back door creaks open. We freeze, eyes wide.

Someone has entered the house.

Go, Blossom mouths, nodding toward the side door. I am prepared to make a run for it when Charlie's mother Claudia enters the living room. She brushes a dark curl behind her ear, brown eyes filled with tears. But she's not looking at me. Her eyes are on her son, still looking very dead on the couch. A tear rolls down the tan skin of her cheek.

"Charlie," she murmurs.

"Sleeping pills," I explain.

Claudia nods. "You've done the right thing."

Relief fills me. "I wish I didn't—"

But Claudia shushes me. She sits on the floor next to the couch, takes Charlie's hand in her own, pressing it to her lips. She looks up at me. "Take your baby," Claudia says. "I'll be here with mine."

"Yes, Faye. Go," Blossom says. "We'll hold them off as long as we can." When Claudia nods her affirmation, Blossom's relief is palpable.

I hug my sister, though it's awkward with Jonas between us. Blossom kisses the top of his head.

"Love you both," she says.

"You too," I say.

I go to Claudia then, kneel on the floor. We embrace each other. She smells of rosemary and sandalwood. "Thank you," I whisper in her ear.

"My son is wrong," she says.

I pull away and touch the tears on her cheek, my own eyes spilling over. "He loves you," I say.

"He does," Claudia says. "But I love my grandson. Go. Save him."

I stand and wipe the tears from my cheeks. I take one last look at Charlie, protected by his mother, and Blossom, looking over mine.

"Okay," I say. "Goodbye."

I slip out through the back door with Jonas, my stomach churning with guilt and gratitude. Hopefully, by the time my mother and Charlie awaken, we will be long gone.

Or, at least, we will have a head start.

It's better than nothing.

It has to be.

I head toward the trailhead. It is blacker now with the deepening night. The mouth is open. It beckons.

The Forest

CHAPTER FOUR
BEFORE THE FOREST

I TURNED A piece of popcorn in my fingers, which had begun to sweat. Arrow was still picking at the label on his beer bottle, avoiding my eyes. Sibling love is complicated.

I cocked my head and squeezed the popcorn piece between my forefinger and thumb, then flicked it with my middle finger. He ducked out of the way, but my aim was as good as his, if not better, and Arrow's aim was keen.

The popcorn landed right between his eyes and the impact penetrated the tension between us. The three of us laughed, as only siblings who have played and fought as fiercely as the three of us could.

"How about my classic town steward aim?" I said and giggled. At least my laugh was genuine.

Arrow held up his hands. "Alright, alright, I concede. Not bad for an old married mom."

This time I plucked a piece of popcorn from the giant bowl at the center of the table and chucked it at him before he even had a chance to flinch. Next thing I knew the three of us were in a full-blown popcorn fight and that's when our mother decided to enter the room. Her timing had always been impeccable. I used to think she was psychic, but now I knew the truth: she was just a mother.

We ceased our popcorn fight and the last few popped

kernels rained onto the hardwood floor like soft puffs of snow.

My mother's hands were on her hips, but her eyes were laughing. She surveyed our mess. We reverted back to children. We sat frozen like baby raccoons caught in a beam of light.

"What's all this about?" Her voice was mock scolding but there was laughter in it. This was her favorite time of year.

There was a soft dusting of flour on her dark blue slacks that betrayed her day spent baking. On anyone else the puff of flour would look messy, but somehow my mother still looked as put together. Her frame was wiry and strong, thin but not frail. Her straight brown hair was streaked with silver and pulled back into a neat, low bun at the nape of her neck. No matter the occasion my mother was calm, assured, and measured. Every move was calculated, considered.

I stuffed an offending bit of popcorn into my mouth and shrugged, then pointed at Arrow. "He started it."

"Hey!" Arrow cracked another bit of popcorn at me, but he was grinning. The tension between us disbursed, but I knew it's still there—always there, like sediment at the bottom of the lake. It settled to the bottom, undisturbed, but it hadn't gone anywhere.

Our mother bent to pick up the pieces of popcorn by her feet. Then she moved to my back and reached down for the garland in front of me, stringing those bits of popcorn onto it. "They're looking good."

Blossom beamed. "Just a couple more batches."

Mom nodded. "Agreed. Thank you all for doing it—even if you are a bunch of rascals."

Blossom held her hand up. "Don't look at me, I had no part in this."

My mouth dropped open in mock incredulity. "Excuse me, missy, but I'm pretty sure I saw a few kernels flying from your direction."

"Who, me?" Blossom fluttered her thick, golden-brown eyelashes at me. "*Never*."

"Well, I for one am glad you're having fun." Mom kissed the top of my head and I inhaled her spiced scent.

She reached for my chin, turned my face gently so I was looking up at her. "How you doing, Faye-baby?"

Blossom and Arrow were watching and my cheeks flamed. I gave my mother my widest smile. "Good." Bright exterior. Don't let the pain show through. She tilted her head, her eyes narrowed ever so slightly.

"How's my baby?" I hoped it sounded like an afterthought but I wasn't able to keep all the purple-tinged panic from my voice.

"He's still asleep in the—oh, speak of the devil," Mom said, because Charlie entered the room with Jonas in the baby carrier.

I intended to stand, but Charlie waved. "Stay. He's good," he said, and it took everything in me to stay put. He sat carefully at the table next to me.

Jonas slept against Charlie's chest, his soft brown baby curls a downy wonder. I stooped slightly to kiss his cheek. The relief that flooded through me was a drug, warm and thick and dizzying. I leaned my head onto Charlie's broad shoulder. I breathed in the soap and cedar scent of him and continued stringing popcorn onto my garland. Mom sat next to Arrow and started helping him with his popcorn string.

"I can't believe he's sleeping through all this," I whispered to Charlie.

"White noise," Charlie replied. His breath against my hair made my neck tingle. "We should get him home soon. What do you think?"

"Yes," I said. "We're just finishing up."

Mom smiled from across the table. "Don't worry, Charlie, we'll let our girl go soon." She tousled Arrow's hair as she would a small boy's. "If these three scoundrels can behave."

18

Blossom surveyed the table. "We're ahead of schedule." She squealed. Her excitement was contagious and my tensed muscles relaxed. Blossom's enthusiasm beamed like light from her eyes. "I *love* the festival."

Mom nodded. "It's the best time of year."

Dad entered the kitchen, book in hand and glasses slipped down toward the tip of his nose. "Sure smells good." He stopped next to Charlie to smooth his hand across Jonas' fuzzy head of hair.

"Dad," I scolded. "You'll wake him."

My warning was futile, because of course he didn't stop, and anyway, Jonas continued on sleeping. His mouth hung wide open, heart-shaped, his breath a soft hushing sound that further eased my inner tension.

Dad reached into the cabinet for a mug. "Any coffee left?"

"Should be plenty." Mom rolled her eyes, but she was smiling. "You seem to be having *quite* the relaxing evening."

Dad shrugged his shoulders to his ears, a goofy defensive gesture, and pointed with one finger at the book in his other hand. "Important work here. Prepping for my speech."

Mom joined him next to the cabinets. "I'm teasing." She kissed his cheek. "Your speeches are always wonderful."

I might have been imagining it, but it seemed like Mom's gaze flickered in my direction before she leaned in to whisper in his ear.

My neck prickled with heat and I turned to catch Blossom's eyes on me. She looked away quickly and smiled, almost too energetic. A quick rush of guilt flooded through me. I'd been shutting her out and she must have felt it. We'd never kept secrets from each other, but my anxiety was barely containable, a feral animal. I was afraid if I let it out, it would destroy the entire town.

"So," Blossom said to anyone at the table who would listen. "What are your sacrifices this year?"

The Forest

CHAPTER FIVE
PRESENT

T HE WOODS AT night are anything but silent.

The forest is alive with the rustling of leaves in the black-night wind, the creaking of tree trunks, the molten liquid rush of the river. There are other sounds, too, sounds that aren't merely vegetable and mineral. Animal sounds. The snapping of branches. The rustling of small and large bodies moving through dried leaves on the forest floor.

Squirrels, and chipmunks. Mice, I tell myself. Raccoons. Possums.

These I can live with.

I try not to think about what else might be walking alongside us in these dark woods. What other kinds of bodies might occupy the forest at night.

I make my way down the bank to the river's edge. I have thought about this long and hard, and while the forest floor would be easier going and would allow me to gain more ground, there are too many nature survivalists in my town. Charlie, of course. My parents and Arrow. They all know how to find and follow a trail. I am pursued by my family. My stomach twists. The people I love. The people I would have done anything to protect.

Almost anything.

I am too weighted down with Jonas and the backpack

to avoid snapping twigs and crushing leaves. My heavy weight leaves deep imprints in the dirt and mud.

There is only one way to ensure my tracks are covered.

I reach the steep part of the bank and have no choice but to execute a controlled slide the rest of the way to the water's edge. One hand grips the walking stick, uses it for leverage on my way down. The other hand protects the back of Jonas' head, in the event of a fall.

I don't fall. At the water's edge, I remove my backpack.

I untie my hiking boots and pull them off. I loop the laces together and knot them. I remove my socks, stuff them into my boots. Push them all the way down to the toes.

Next I remove my pants. I roll them up. I unzip my backpack and shove my pants inside. After I zip my pack, I tie my boots to the strap on its top. I stand carefully and hoist it onto my shoulders.

Shivering now, I face the river. The cool night air chills my bare legs and toes.

I try not to think about the black river water, and what might lie beneath its rippling surface.

For Jonas. He is still sound asleep, making soft little snoring sounds. I kiss the top of his head.

I step into the water and gasp.

It's colder than I expected. There are smooth stones beneath the water's surface, interspersed with patches of soft, squishy mud. The feel of the mud beneath my feet is upsetting. I have the sudden thought that slimy bodies might be burrowed within it. I wade forward despite these unsettling fantasies.

The current moves in the direction that I need to go. The water here is just under my knees, but I move carefully. This river stays manageable for a while, but after the years I spent playing in it every summer, I know that there are sudden drops.

I remember back to those warm, golden-sunlight

dappled summers, so beautiful the memory hurts with its sharp edges. They seem so long ago, right now. The forest of my childhood was a different place, somewhere far away from the dark, unfriendly place I now find myself in.

Another bitter pill of betrayal to swallow

Not even the forest is what I'd believed it to be.

My eyes are beginning to adjust to the darkness. The forest is pale and shimmering, with shades of black and grey and muted white. The nighttime landscape is more muted, its usually vivid color faded, nearly nonexistent.

Jonas snores softly, a kitten purring, and I run my hand along the curve of his back. Though the water isn't deep, I am trudging. The water sloshes around my legs, my hand tired of gripping the walking stick against the pull of the current. The rippling water echoes loudly through the forest and I feel vulnerable in the open. Conspicuous. I hear sounds along the water's edge, not all of them benign. What stalks me?

My favorite movie as a child was *The Wizard of Oz*. "There's no place like home," Dorothy said, and I'd tried so hard to believe it.

Rustling sounds along the riverbank taunt my ears. Every sound is enhanced, amplified in these dark woods. My eyes strain to see in the dark, but I can't make out anything clearly. Only vague shapes and deep black pockets that hide everything.

Squirrels. Chipmunks. Raccoons. Oh, my.

These are better than the alternatives.

I caress the hard outline of Charlie's knife in my pocket and feel a little safer.

Of course, I have never killed anything besides insects. I've never hunted. I don't know if I could take a life.

Jonas makes a soft squeaking noise that echoes in the dark.

***

I feel like I've been walking forever, but when I check my

digital watch, it's only been about an hour. Despite my best attempts to evenly distribute the weight I'm carrying, my back and shoulders ache. My stomach grumbles. I've caught my head nodding a few times, a thought that scares me in this murky black water.

I pause and retrieve the water bottle that hangs from my backpack strap. I drink deeply. I hadn't realized I was so thirsty. The cool water feels good against my throat. I am warm from my exertions, despite the cold river's numbing effect on my calves and shins. I replace my water bottle and continue my trudge.

Haven't I gone far enough? Haven't I thrown them off long enough? How much longer should I walk in the river?

As far as I can. Until I can't.

I steel my shoulders, grit my teeth, keep walking forward.

But I'm not being as careful as I was before. My senses are dull with fatigue and I'm just going through the motions. I'm not paying close enough attention to the river's gritty surface beneath. I realize this, and yet—

Suddenly I am submerged in shoulder length, icy cold water. Jonas' head is beneath the water's surface.

The backpack provides an uneven buoyancy that makes it difficult for me to find my footing. It lifts my feet from the bottom of the river. My toes thrash in the water, looking to find purchase on the river's edge.

My baby. His head is still underwater.

I try not to panic, but this is impossible.

The cold current wraps icy fingers around my body, tugs and pulls.

Jonas.

I grit my teeth.

My feet finally find the bottom of the river. With all the strength that's in me, I bend my knees and shove myself toward the right bank. The backpack makes my movements wobbly and lopsided, but the water is shallower here and I regain my balance. I push myself up to stand, see the top of Jonas' head, his soft wet hair.

His sharp, mewling cry echoes in the dark night.

The water is to my thighs, now to my knees, now my ankles.

Then I am standing on the riverbank, water dripping from my clothes. My breath is shaky and uneven, but I am not as cold as I would have expected. The night air feels warm compared to the biting cold of the water.

Jonas cries louder now, and coughs. My stomach twists at the thought of water in his lungs. What if I hadn't made it out? What if we'd been swept away? What if I had killed him?

I realize with a cold jolt that I must be beyond Edgewood's borders and the two stone pillars that denote it. I draw in a shaky breath. I have only been outside the boundaries once before, but I can't bear to remember. Not now, not here. Not after what just happened. What I do know is that I need to be exceedingly cautious from here on out. We are not under Edgewood's protection, now.

The abyss yawns.

I feel it sucking at me, black and yearning, pulling me down, down.

I can't think these thoughts.

I yearn for Edgewood's safety and then I cringe. That safety was not real, was not true, was bought with my sister's blood. This thought fills me up with silent rage that simmers into quiet resolve. I will keep going. I will do this.

Jonas' cries make me feel exposed, vulnerable. His warm, wet body clings to mine. I cup my shaky hand around the back of his head, press my lips to his wet hair. "Shhhh, baby, you're okay," I whisper. "Mommy's here. Mommy's so sorry. Mommy should have been more careful."

We need to get dry. I feel warm, for now, but that won't last when my body temperature readjusts. The night breeze is already cooling my damp skin. I need to get Jonas into dry clothes. I need to find a safe place to rest.

I climb out of the riverbank and enter the forest. Fortune is with us. At least, I think.

I hope.

Because, after half a mile, I see a shadowy structure in the middle of the wood.

My stomach knots with apprehension.

It is a crude, manmade structure. A small hut constructed out of branches, twisted and tangled together around the sturdy trunk of a tree.

Who built this?

Why is it here?

I feel far away from town. What if I'm not as far as I think I am?

But Jonas is shivering, and I don't really have a choice. I need to get us changed and warm and dry.

I hoist the backpack from my shoulders, place it on the ground. Once we are inside, I reach through the door, and drag my backpack inside.

It's dark in the hut. There is the faint smell of decay, the mildew smell of rotting leaves. I unzip the backpack with fingers that are stiffening from cold.

I reach inside and feel a rush of gratitude for Charlie's obsessive and unnecessary wilderness survival preparation. The backpack has lived up to its name, and the contents are completely dry. The inside of my boots is wet, of course. I expose their insides to the night air, hoping they'll dry as much as possible before morning.

I fish around blindly inside and finally find the flashlight and click it on. I think of the light leaking through the tangled branches of the hut. The thought of what might be looking in from the forest makes me shudder. What might be able to see us, now that this light has exposed our position. I try not to think about it.

After I changed Jonas' diaper and dressed him in

warm, dry clothes, I lay one of our blankets on the shelter's bare dirt floor and place Jonas on his back. He is wide awake, now, and his large dark eyes take in our strange surroundings.

When finished, I lay our clothes flat to dry. Next to Jonas, I pull my knees into my chest and sweep the flashlight around the hut's interior.

It's not very big, a six-foot circumference at the most. It doesn't look like any humans have been here for a very long time. There are no food wrappers, or bottles or cans. Nothing to indicate anyone has been here recently. It feels abandoned.

But then, everything seems abandoned at night.

And humans aren't my only worry. I don't know if we are saved here, or if we are waiting in a trap.

My flashlight snags on something in the opposite end of the structure. A small mound, a pile of some kind.

My back prickles. I glance quickly at Jonas, who is sound asleep on the soft blanket.

In the darkness, I move closer.

At first, it looks like a heap of greyish sticks, carefully stacked and piled. Deliberately placed there.

Deliberately placed there.

By whom?

My heart is racing now, and still, I move closer to the sticks.

Not sticks, but bones.

Bones.

I bend to get a closer look.

Chicken bones.

Chicken *leg* bones.

My blood oscillates between hot and cold. I think of Bobby Perkins and his chickens that went missing in the night.

These are pieces to a puzzle, but so many are missing.

I lean in.

The Forest

The stench of forest rot is stronger now.

In the mound of bones, there are bits of flesh and tendon and dried blood still stuck to them.

Who stacked them here?

Whose hut is this?

Who?

I have the sudden, horrible feeling that I am being watched and click off my flashlight.

I rush back to Jonas, press my hands to the warmth of his sleeping body and try to calm my shaky, uneven breathing.

Exhaustion overwhelms me.

I could walk for miles and not find a shelter this good. Jonas and I both need sleep. My mind is playing tricks on me. I don't know what's real, who or what or where I'm supposed to trust.

I close my eyes, try to feel around for answers.

My gut tells me this is safe, deep down, despite the earthy mildew smell and the chicken bones. For tonight, anyway, we are safe. We are far enough away from town, and without having left any immediate tracks, our whereabouts are a mystery for now.

If I am going to be my best for Jonas, I need to sleep. The hardest part is done. We left. We made it out.

Now we just need to evade our pursuers long enough to escape this forest.

I think of my wet boots, tongues open to the night air. If we need to run, pulling my boots on will waste precious time. But walking in wet boots tomorrow will be terrible for my feet. I decide to chance it and let them dry as much as possible while we sleep.

I lay on my side and pull Jonas close, offering him my breast. He latches. His warm body curls against mine. A surge of gratitude fills me and I soften into the natural comfort of our dyad. I pull the second blanket over our two bodies, careful to keep his face uncovered.

I've camped before, but never alone—or, never almost alone, never with a small baby to protect. On those camping trips, I never realized how loud the forest is at night. Alive with crickets, with creaking, with rustling, with twigs snapping and popping.

What is out there?

Or whom.

Is something (someone) watching us?

Who?

Don't think about it now.

Don't.

We are safe.

I have to believe that. I have to *feel* it. I *do* feel it.

I am driven by something stronger than emotion, something more powerful than knowledge or fear or anger or hate. Stronger even than love.

I am driven by my mother's instinct.

I curl my body closer into my sweet baby. His suckles transition to the light flutters of a nursling who's drifted into sleep.

I close my eyes and listen to the sounds of the forest. I am very alone, and my body swells with sadness.

None of this is what I wanted.

What I wouldn't give to find out it was all a dream, to wake up like Dorothy and tell my family, "And you were there, and you, and you, and you." And to sit with them over breakfast and laugh about it, to drink coffee, to eat my mother's heart-warming cookies. To go on with our perfect, happy lives.

They say, "ignorance is bliss"—and now I know why.

It would have been easier just to not know. Easier, but false.

My mind filled with the "knowledge of good and evil," I drift into anxious sleep.

CHAPTER SIX
BEFORE THE FOREST

WHAT ARE YOUR *sacrifices this year?*
Silence bloomed in the wake of Blossom's question. We shuffled around the table, each waiting for the first person willing to volunteer this intimate information.

Blossom's green eyes shone, and she made an exasperated sound in the back of her throat. "Fine, I'll go first. I've been thinking about it a lot, and I'm going to give the bundle of dried flowers I collected from my section of the garden last spring."

Arrow rolled his eyes. "It has to really *mean* something, Bud." Blossom gave him a scathing look at the use of her childhood nickname. "You know that."

"It does mean something, you derp," she said, teeth gritted. "Those flowers were the first I ever grew completely myself, from seed to bloom."

"Do they mean as much to you as that necklace?" Arrow gestured to the silver locket strung with a delicate chain around Blossom's neck.

Blossom's hand flew to the necklace, cheeks flushing pinker than usual. "I do *love* this necklace," she said, a little too quickly. "But the *flowers* represent me and my hard work. Something I did on my own."

"I guess the necklace just represents your undying love

for Josie Miller." Arrow's intense eyes burned with the fire of pure mischief.

"Shut up," Blossom mumbled and stabbed a piece of popcorn.

"What did that popcorn ever do to you?" I squeezed Blossom's arm again. She looked at me from the corner of her eye, cheeks still rose-red, and I grinned.

"The flowers are a lovely choice," I said. "And meaningful. That's what matters to the fire, right? It's not the cost of the thing, or who gave it to you. It's about you and your own abundance. However that manifests."

"It also has to hurt." It was Arrow's own particularly warped interpretation of the rule that we must choose something *meaningful*. He turned to me. "So, what are you giving?"

It was my turn to flush. "Jonas' first newborn outfit."

They didn't have children, so they couldn't truly understand what that might mean to me, but a collective nod rippled around the table. They accepted the answer; it was believable, because I meant it to be. The conversation around me continued as the others talked of their sacrifices, while I thought of the old maps still hidden beneath my bed. I struggled to quell the guilt that rose like sickness in the back of my throat.

I swallowed it down, but my stomach soured. My postpartum anxiety, a thing that shouldn't be possible in Edgewood, felt so pointedly like punishment. It was my shameful secret, but it was my burden to bear. Was it because I'd been dishonest with the fire? Did the fire *know*? Did the land? What else would it ask of me, what worse things would it take, besides my sense of peace?

I took a deep, shaky breath. Tonight would be one of the bad nights. I thought of the sleeping pills Charlie's mother quietly obtained for me, tucked safely into the back of my nightstand drawer. My mouth watered with longing for the temporary relief I knew they'd bring me.

30

Anxiety roiled within me, filled me up with tiny worms of darkness.

"Did we lose you again?" Blossom whispered, her breath hot against my ear.

"What?" I pressed my forehead against her cheek. "No. Sorry. I'm here. I am."

I felt Arrow looking at me, eyes blazing as ever. He opened his mouth but before he could speak, there was a loud knock on the front door.

I could not say why, but the knock filled me with dread.

It was silly to feel that way just two days before the festival. It was normal for people to be stopping by amidst the craze of preparation. Even so, the worms of anxiety that churned through my belly began to writhe like snakes.

My dad set his book and coffee mug down on the kitchen counter.

The conversation at the table continued, with arguments and defenses about sacrifice choices whirring into a cacophony of noise. The individual words escaped me despite my feeble attempts to listen; I tried to pin my focus onto stabbing the needle through each individual popcorn to create the garland, but my guts were a mess. The snakes continued to grow and churn, moving as though to poise, ready to strike. As though I was waiting.

And I was.

Sharp and clear through the din in the dining room, my father cried out:

"Lois, come here?"

The tenor of alarm in his voice set the tangle of snakes in my belly to biting.

CHAPTER SEVEN
PRESENT

THERE IS SOMETHING outside the hut.
Something big.
Sniffing. Huffing.

Sunrise leaks in through the cracks of the branches, and my eyes strain to see outside. The branches are tangled together well, though. Whoever built this shelter was skilled, wanted it to last.

Jonas is still sleeping.

Movement through the cracks. A large body brushes up against the hut's "walls." Light brown fur.

It's a deer.

I exhale, slowly. I hadn't even realized I'd been holding my breath.

I poke my head out of the entrance of the shelter. The deer freezes; stares at me. I lift my hand.

"Hello," I whisper. "We won't hurt you."

I reach toward the deer and she bolts.

I dip my head and slip back inside the shelter.

Jonas stirs, then stretches all of his limbs, yawns. His mouth makes a perfect pink "O"; revealing the gummy ridges of his jawline. He only has one tooth, on the bottom. Even here, in this hut in the middle of the forest, in these frightening circumstances, all I want to do is watch him. When he finishes yawning and stretching, he settles back into sleep. His bottom lip looks fat when he sleeps, and the tip of his tiny tongue nearly always sticks out of his mouth.

I watch him sleep, and I want to freeze this moment. The sunlight that splashes in through these makeshift walls is rich and golden, alive in the way that light only is at the beginning and the end of the day. I hear the babble of the river, the morning birdsongs. The skittering and scampering of tiny woodland critters. And my son snoring softly in the midst of it all, his body framed by the soft red and black checkered blanket beneath him.

If I don't think about why we're out here, this is the kind of picturesque moment that happens so rarely in regular life. It's almost something from a postcard.

Minus the fact that my hair is a dark, matted mess after our encounter with the river last night. I must look a sight.

I shake my head.

No.

I can't become complacent.

I can't allow the lull of the forest, my childhood happy place, to trick me into letting my guard down. I can't forget why we're out here. Why we had to leave. Who might be after us. Who might be in the forest with us, already.

The forest isn't what I'd always believed it to be.

The forest is not my friend.

It won't protect Jonas.

We aren't safe.

Not yet.

The morning air is sharp and fresh and cool and I drink it in. It tastes sweet, like earth and pine and sunlight. And I can't help but think again how very beautiful the forest is in the morning light, and how mysterious, that the forest's secrets seem so much more dangerous at night.

Before Jonas wakes, I ready myself. I eat some cereal bars and an apple sauce packet. I drink half of my water bottle, careful to savor it, careful not to gulp too quickly. I need to make it last. I'm not really looking forward to swallowing bottlefuls of purified river water.

I check our clothes and my boots from last night. They are still damp, though not drenched. They need more time to fully dry, but that will have to be later. Today, I must put as much ground between us and Edgewood as possible. I roll up my clothes and tuck them into the bottom of the backpack, reorganizing the bag as I do so.

The baby carrier is also damp, but it will dry in the forest air while we walk.

Just as I'm finished getting myself situated, Jonas wakes.

"Good morning, sunshine," I whisper. I am anxious to get moving, but I don't want him to feel it. "Something special for you today, little love. Breakfast on the go."

Jonas' eyes light up and he rolls onto his belly, bounces up and down.

"You like that?" I croon. "You want to nurse while we walk? That's fun!"

He babbles happily and I move him off the blanket so I can fold it and return it to my backpack. I can't stand fully upright in the hut, so I drag the pack and baby carrier out through the shelter's opening. I retrieve the compass and secure the baby carrier around my waist. Then I go back into the shelter for Jonas.

Back outside the hut, I place him into the carrier with his belly pressed to mine. Once I have the carrier's straps secured and the backpack in place, I lift my shirt. Jonas nurses as I walk, his cheek against my sternum.

The compass guides my steps. I need to go Northeast. The forest is long, sprawling, expansive—but I know that the main road wraps around it. If I walk long enough, and in the right direction, we will eventually find the other side of the road. And from there, the nearest town is not too far. I will either walk, or we will find a ride.

There is always the possibility that they will be waiting

for me on the road, though it's unlikely. For one, they won't have a clear way of knowing exactly where we will emerge from the forest.

And besides that, even if they *could* pinpoint exactly where we'd emerge, it would likely be after the Equinox. And if we miss the ceremony, it will be too late for their bargain.

No. They won't want to risk choosing the wrong exit point, or wasting their time waiting for something that may not happen in time. They will want to find us before the Equinox, so there is still time to offer Jonas to the forest.

Their best bet is to track us through the forest, from behind.

I look around at the tall trees, the fading green and yellow leaves not yet turned to the jeweled brilliance of fall.

Jonas is, after all, already in the forest.

I try not to think about what that could mean.

I could be playing the forest's hand. This could be a trap.

He suckles and nuzzles against me, making sweet, soft swallowing sounds. I grit my teeth.

I look again to the lush shrubbery, the tangled branches, the tall trees, the light filtering in between canopy and trunks.

"Over my dead body," I whisper.

To no one, but also to the forest. To whoever might be listening. Whatever—*whoever*—might be following.

The forest doesn't answer me, of course.

Branches snap beneath my feet, dried leaves crunch. Birds sing. Squirrel scamper, dart across my path and up tree trunks.

It's still so beautiful, I think. Beautiful as ever. The place I feel the most at home.

Home.

I feel another stab of betrayal, the sting of loss upon loss.

LISA QUIGLEY

There's no place like home.
But where is home, now?

Jonas unlatches, looks up at me from the carrier with wide, curious eyes.

I help him access my other breast, press his cheek against my chest, kiss the top of his soft head.

Home is wherever I'm with you.

MY PARENTS HAD not yet returned from answering the knock at the door.

I made eye contact with Charlie when my mother hurried from the room to answer my father's call. Charlie's dark brown eyes mirrored my concern, if not the poisonous anxiety that coursed through me. Something wasn't right.

Tension built in the room. Our popcorn garlands were forgotten. Blossom had tensed beside me.

Arrow's brow was creased. "What is it?" he said.

"Could be anything," I said. "It's festival time."

"Then why do you look like that?" Arrow said.

"Like what?"

"Like you ate something sour."

I shrugged. "I'm sure it's nothing."

But then my mother appeared in the kitchen doorway. Her face was drawn, eyes solemn. My fears were confirmed the minute I saw her: something *was* wrong.

"Faye, Charlie, come here, please?"

"What is it?" I said.

My mother shook her head, a definitive movement. "A steward matter."

Charlie and I were not town stewards yet, but we would be in a matter of days. My parents had been including us in town matters for months in preparation. It wasn't unusual for them to consult our judgment or involve us in town issues. What *was* unusual was the way my mother rubbed her hands together, the way the corners of her mouth were pinned too tightly against the sides of her face.

We stood, and I pressed my hand quickly to Jonas' back in the baby carrier. He was still sound asleep.

When we reached the front door, my mother opened it, ushered us out onto the front porch, and quickly shut it again.

My father was on the front porch with Bobby Perkins, who was holding a shoebox—the sight of which filled me with more of that poisonous foreboding. Charlie placed a hand on the small of my back. Jonas' snored softly, oblivious to anything amiss in the cadence of our lives.

Bobby Perkins' expression was one of downright panic. He'd been worried about his missing chickens; it was a small thing, almost negligible, that in any other place would simply be par for the course. But in Edgewood? It was worse than unlucky. We'd grown accustomed to good fortune and this unsettling bit of bad luck had both perplexed and frightened us. And it had weighed heavily on my conscience. Something was wrong with me—that much was clear. I was broken, and who knew what else had broken along with me. What I had let in.

I forced myself to stop looking at Bobby to glance at my father. His grey eyes were stormy.

"What is it?" I said again.

"There's something you need to see." My father nodded at Bobby.

With clear hesitation, Bobby removed the shoe box lid, tilted it to catch the porchlight so Charlie and I could see the contents.

The chicken was mangled and bloody. Its death was not an accident. That much was blatantly obvious. The chicken's legs were gone, angry red wounds in their place.

I covered my mouth with my hand. "What—how—?"

But I couldn't finish my thought. Saying it out loud would make it even more real than the mangle of flesh and blood in the box before my eyes that *should've* been impossible in Edgewood.

"Found her this way," Bobby said, voice shaky.

"What's it mean?" Charlie said.

My mother shook her head, mouth a thin line. "We can't be sure, yet."

"This . . . can't happen." I could barely speak. "Who would—do such a thing? Here? How is it even possible?"

My father wrapped his arm around Bobby's shoulder. "Listen, Bobby, we'd appreciate it if you'd keep this quiet, for now."

"You don't want me to tell anyone? Warn anyone? What if—heck, I don't know. What if we're in danger?"

My mother moved close to Bobby, too. "We understand your concern, truly," she said, voice soft but firm. "But until we—well, we need some time to get a handle on this. To look into it. If word gets out, the town could go into a panic which would only muddy matters."

Bobby nodded, but I could see he was reluctant. He was questioning everything he understood to be true, as I knew we all were.

It was not just that people didn't do bad things in Edgewood, or that terrible things didn't happen. It's that they *couldn't*. This was the guarantee. It's what made Edgewood sacred. It's what we purchased every year with our gifts to the fire.

I took a deep breath. "The festival is in two days. The sacrifice will put everything right."

"How can you be sure?" Bobby was trembling, and I didn't blame him.

"That's the way it works."

"Pure evil," Bobby said. "Chickens gone missing, now, that was cause for concern. But a deliberately mangled chicken left in my coup? That is malicious. This wasn't a wild animal. This could only have been done by a—"

But he stopped because to think it was terrible, but to speak it was abhorrent. He didn't need to say it out loud though, because we were all thinking it. The only thing that could have done such a thing, in so violent and precise a way, was another *human*.

While we did kill animals in Edgewood, it was always done with reverence and gratitude, in a manner that was quick and humane. We used as much of the animals as we could, and we certainly didn't kill for entertainment.

This was worse than even sport. This was aggression. Menace.

"Is my family even safe?" Bobby's face twisted into an anguished contortion.

My father reached forward and gently pressed the shoebox lid closed. "Bobby," he said, his voice low and persuasive. "Won't you give us some time to think on this a bit? We'll call Sheriff Wilson, ask him to send a couple of his deputies to patrol outside your house."

Bobby nodded. "Yeah, alright."

We didn't really have the need for law enforcement in our town, but we had always had a small sheriff's department. More out of tradition, a formality, than actual necessity. I doubted that his deputies would even know what to do in the event of a real threat, given that they'd had zero actual experience with life-or-death matters. I kept these thoughts to myself.

My dad took the shoebox from Bobby, who relinquished it. "We'll hang onto this."

Bobby looked relieved to be free of the thing.

Mom squeezed Bobby's shoulders, gently. "Go on home, Bobby. Try to rest up. Relax and prepare for the festival. We will figure this mess out. It's our job, not yours."

Bobby still appeared shaken but seemed calm for the moment. We said goodnight and he left.

My father headed to the garage with the shoebox. I leaned in to kiss the top of Jonas' head. He was still sleeping soundly and blissfully unaware of our current predicament.

"We should get him in bed," I said, and shuddered. "Though I don't know if I'll be able to sleep tonight. Not after—that."

My mother was watching me acutely, a funny look on her face that I couldn't place.

"Mom," I said, suddenly uncertain. "What is it?"

"Your father and I need to talk to you. Both of you. Tomorrow evening? I'll make dinner."

"Now I really won't sleep. Can't we just talk now?"

My mother held my gaze and still, I couldn't place what it was that made her eyes shine with such strange light. "I would rather we talk to the two of you alone," she said. She meant without Blossom and Arrow. "It's . . . steward business. And it's important."

I shrugged and took Charlie's hand. It was a warm night but I felt suddenly chilled. "Sure, of course," I said.

Charlie squeezed my hand. "No problem."

"We really should go," I said.

My mother nodded. "Blossom and Arrow can finish up the garlands. Just get that one home."

My father returned from the garage and we all headed back inside together. Charlie and I gathered our things and said goodnight to my family.

I felt detached from my body. My stomach writhed with anxiety and my blood pumped too quickly. I was dizzy, nervous, numb. A skittish animal, ready to bolt into the bordering forest at the slightest provocation, about to drown in angry white waters of a hungry river.

I took deep breaths, but they couldn't compete with my racing heart or the frantic tangle of dark thoughts that ravaged me, climbing like hungry weeds along the inside of my skull. I went through the motions, saying what I was supposed to say, returned kisses, but inside I was not there. Our last moments in the house blurred together into a haze of disjointed images.

It was as though I was somewhere far away, like I was floating above and beyond my body. On the walk back to our own home, I was drowning in the sewage of my internal landscape.

There was only one detail I remembered, inconsequential as it may have been; one thing I kept replaying over and over.

My mother hadn't kissed Jonas goodnight.

CHAPTER NINE
PRESENT

I WALK UNTIL NOON. We have covered a lot of ground without incident. I have stayed alert, my eyes open and listening for sounds, for voices, for footsteps. Any hint that they are following, that they are getting close.

But I hear nothing.

This worries me.

It also heartens me, makes me hope maybe we will make it. There is too much forest, too few of them. Jonas and me, we are just the two of us. Two needles in a massive haystack. They won't know where to start. We will make it to the forest edge, to the road, to the next town. We will find help, law enforcement, a hospital, a shelter, something, somewhere, anywhere. I will explain our predicament, tell what these people—my town, my community, my friends, my family—wanted me to do.

It's criminal.

We will be helped. We will be protected. We will survive.

My mounting hope, the intensity of it: this is what worries me.

I am afraid it will make me careless. Complacent.

So, I overcompensate.

Every noise startles me. Every shuffle of squirrels, of chipmunks. Every snap and pop of twigs. Every rustle.

Every movement in the corner of my eye. I am jumpy. I have to be. To keep us safe. To protect Jonas.

Despite my high alert, my mind does wander occasionally. I find myself thinking about the shelter we found. Who built it? How long has it been there? These questions perplex, intrigue, and frighten me.

It was probably built by teenagers, set free for the summer. *Teenagers from where?* It was likely a clubhouse of sorts, a place to gather in the woods, share secrets and stories.

Or maybe it was a parental project. A mother and a father built a play hut for their children.

These are the most likely answers.

But, all the way out here? So far from the edge of town?

The thought of that empty shelter, living a secret life out here in the forest, occupied from time to time with . . . with what? With *whom*?

My stomach twists.

The abyss yawns.

We take a short break to eat lunch and to give my shoulders reprieve. Then I continue walking. For a while, I turn Jonas to face out in the baby carrier, so he will be entertained by the forest greenery and creatures. By the sights and sounds and smells. He is beginning to wiggle and struggle against the carrier. He is tired of walking; I don't blame him. My shoulders ache.

We walk the rest of the day without incident.

I am surprised, and suspicious. I want to keep walking, but I am weary. It is dusk and my back is screaming. I don't want to set up camp in the dark.

I begin looking for a place where we can rest. Where we will be hidden and protected.

Finally, I see a nest of thickly clustered bushes and trees. Not a manmade shelter this time, but that is actually a relief.

No, this natural mass of tangled shrubbery will work

nicely. It offers not only shelter, but camouflage. It's almost completely enclosed on all sides, and in the center is a small clearing with just enough space for Jonas and me to sleep. There is a small opening, but we will be relatively hidden from the view of any curious animals, or anyone who might be looking for us. And whatever else might be lurking in the forest.

The trees overhead creak in the cool autumn breeze.

Is the forest aware of our presence?

I have always felt that the forest is a living thing, an entity unto itself. The idea used to thrill me, to fill me with a sense of wonder and curiosity.

But now the thought is upsetting. I may have run away from those who wish to harm us, and headed right into the open arms of a worse monster.

It might already be over.

The darkness beckons.

I shake the backpack from my shoulders, a nearly unbearable relief. I rub my shoulders, then shove the pack into the burrow. Tonight is cooler than last night, but inside our little shelter we are shielded from the harsh fall air. I lay a blanket on the hard ground, pull out the second. I change Jonas' diaper and bury the soiled one in the dirt, whispering apologies to the earth.

Jonas nurses while I munch fruit and granola bars. He has been so good so far, barely fussing or crying. He has loved being outside, ever since he was a newborn. I am grateful for this, grateful for his naturally even, mellow disposition. Motherhood sometimes feels like drowning, but Jonas makes a difficult thing easier.

When I finish eating, we curl beneath our blanket and bunker in for the night. I've been worried sleep wouldn't come easily, but my body is weary. I close my eyes, feel my body relax. Listen to the forest sing its night-song.

The forest is vast and full of mystery, and Jonas and I feel so small within it. The thought is a comfort during the day, when we are pursued and the sunlight makes us vulnerable. At night, though, the thought swallows me. We are insignificant, microscopic.

I want all this to mean something. I want our story to have a purpose. But out here, so small in this landscape that doesn't yield itself to us—I fear that's not the case.

My mind troubles over these things, and my eyelids get heavy.

The next time I open my eyes, bright early morning daylight peeks through the branches. The light is mesmerizing: dappled and golden. It feels playful.

I reach up, catch a flicker of sunlight on my palm. I turn my hand over and over, let the sunshine warm me, wake me.

I stretch luxuriously and yawn. I hadn't expected to be able to sleep so well. My body aches, but my mind feels refreshed, prepared for another day.

I reach for Jonas, but Jonas is gone.

46

W E SAT AT the kitchen table in my parents' dining room. My father wouldn't look me in the eye. I resisted a barely-containable urge to run.

Jonas squirmed in my lap, wiggled to break free of my grasp, which had tightened.

Mom had spent her day baking more sweet potato pies in preparation for the fall festival and equinox ceremony. She still had a smudge of flour on her nose, a small detail that felt unbearably domestic against the stark backdrop of the tension in that moment.

My mother's lips began moving, and my body tensed. I squeezed my eyes shut and it did nothing to drown out the sound of her voice. Something terrible was coming. The still air in the kitchen vibrated with it.

"Faye, Charlie," she began, "there's no sense in delaying any further. As you saw last night with Bobby's chicken, the situation is becoming dire."

I nodded. "The festival tomorrow, the fire, that will take care of it. That will—"

But she held up her hand. "The fire is not why we are safe."

The confusion on Charlie's face mirrored my own. "But we do it every year," I said.

My mother nodded. My father kept looking at his hands. "It's easier this way," she said. "Simpler, for them to feel involved. But do you really think that a few treasured goods tossed into a fire would be enough to sustain the magic that makes this town so special?"

My eyes widened. I didn't know what to say. Because, yes, I'd simply believed it to be enough. I'd had no reason not to.

"That isn't the way it works," she continued. "This will be hard for you to hear, but I'm going to just come out and say it. In exchange for protection, the town stewards must offer up their first-born child. The forest demands it."

The air in the kitchen was more still than ever. None of us moved. Her words vibrated like a curse through my body. The black pit that had been pulling at me all those months widened, loomed nearer. It had finally come for me.

"What do you mean, 'offer up'?" My voice sounded too high, like my words were coming from a precarious place. "What does that *mean*?"

My mother sighed. "Perhaps we were unwise in waiting to tell you." She looked at my father, briefly, then back to me. "But I . . . spent my whole life knowing, dreading, waiting. I thought, if I could spare you some of that, allow you to keep your innocence . . . You've always been so—unsure—and I didn't want to—"

"You didn't want me to have a *choice*. You never have."

My mother's gaze was intense. My father was the opposite: eyes looking everywhere but my face; his large, freckled hands clasped tightly together on the wooden tabletop. I was acutely aware of the way Charlie had moved so that his knee was no longer touching mine beneath the table, though I couldn't yet decipher what that meant.

From that angle I could see the treehouse shaped like a pirate ship—affectionately dubbed the *treeship*—through the dining room window. My father helped us build it when

48

we were children. The sight of it—but more than that: the incongruously happy memories it conjured up—made my stomach clench. I looked away.

I hugged Jonas tighter, and he protested.

My mother held my gaze. I was still in disbelief. Her words had spilled from her mouth as though they were something ordinary, like water. Or blood. I could not bring myself to comprehend or, even worse, believe them.

I felt simultaneously disconnected from my body and acutely anchored to the physical reality of the moment. The last time I remembered feeling that way was when I peed on the pregnancy test and those two blue lines appeared. A moment so surreal, when life as I knew it changed forever, when my reality split into two distinct parts. Maiden and mother, converged in a single moment in time.

"You still haven't answered my question," I said.

My mother sighed. "On the eve of the Equinox, during the ceremony, we are to leave Jonas at the forest's edge."

"*Leave* him there? To, what? Die?"

"It is a worthy exchange," my mother said. "A necessary sacrifice."

I shook my head, my mind a cobweb of disbelief. "You're lying," I finally said, though I had never known my mother to be a liar.

My mother's face softened, the laugh lines that deepened around the corners of her eyes adding to the layers of painful betrayal. "What do you think happened to Autumn?" Her words were slow, measured like the ingredients in her baked goods.

Realization hit and the world tilted around me. From some place faraway I recognized that I was still squeezing Jonas too tightly, and he cried out.

"You're hurting him," Charlie said.

Charlie extended his arms to our son and, reflexively, I held him just out of reach.

"Don't." My voice was sharp, a gleaming edge. I was a

mother bear, and I felt my nails growing into claws. I was ready to protect. Prepared to kill.

Charlie's hands dropped. I looked at him, seeking an ally. I have seen him full of fight, back when the cancer was still mercilessly eating away at his mother.

Charlie had only been eighteen years old when he wandered onto an obscure message board on the Internet. It had just been a single comment in a long, meandering thread about mystical health cures. A single comment that mentioned the magic of Edgewood, offering his family last-dash hope. He'd never been able to find the comment again—but that's how Edgewood worked. It was mysterious. You couldn't find it if you went looking for it— but if it wanted to be found, it would find *you*.

Charlie's father thought it was distasteful to believe in such things, to hope in such miracles, and his sister had been dubious, but his mother, a spiritual woman, had believed it to be a sign. She'd been quite literally on death's doorstep and was willing to take a leap of faith. Charlie was, too—seeing his mother being eaten alive from the inside out like that had proven more than he could bear— and he, along with his sister, had helped his mother make the outrageous move.

His father had not.

They'd never really expected that it would work. And when it had . . . when she'd been healed within a matter of weeks, all signs of the cancer gone . . . well. Suffice it to say, they weren't going anywhere.

And then we fell in love, and they *really* weren't going anywhere.

I looked for that fighter there at my parents' table, searched for that fierce protector, my soul mate, but Charlie's gaze was in his lap, his breathing shallow. I decided he must be in shock and disbelief, as I was, but I needed him to look at me. I needed to know that I wasn't alone in the dark. To infer that his avoidance meant anything more was too frightening, and I couldn't allow myself to slip into that place.

"Autumn." My voice was barely a whisper, and a fresh wave of nauseous realization rippled through me, a rock disturbing placid water.

Of course. It had been naïve to believe that anything other than calculated tragedy could befall a family in a place like Edgewood.

Though I never met her, my sister felt like a faint memory, a soft whisper on the chilled fall breeze. A story I'd always wanted to know. But she'd been there in the shadows, and always, always in the Rowan wood necklace around my neck, like a totem. The one my mother gifted me when she told me Autumn's story.

Not the *true* story, I realized.

My hand flew to the necklace, my damp fingertips gripped the smooth beads. Comfort for a comfort-less moment.

My mother's confession congealed in the pit of my belly. We had always celebrated Autumn's life but had never spoken of the details of her death—until now. I had always associated Autumn with the forest, and it chilled me to recognize how right my intuition had been.

"I won't do it," I said now. I turned to Charlie. "Right, babe? *We* won't do it."

But Charlie still wouldn't look at me. Instead, he addressed my mother. "What would happen to her?"

I was confused. *Look at me!* My whole body screamed. "To who? Me? It would destroy me."

Charlie shuffled nervously. "Will it come back?"

My mother's eyes were blue and filled with liquid compassion. I wanted to strangle her. "I don't have an answer," she said. "It's a possibility. We have no way of knowing what will happen—to everyone, to the town—if the deal is not honored."

Jonas was screaming now. Panic was a bubble in my

LISA QUIGLEY

throat, expanding and threatening to burst, to overflow. I lifted my shirt and tilted Jonas on his side, offered him my breast. He latched onto me, his mouth warm, his suction strong, and his sobs turned to content swallows.

"We won't do it," I said again. "Right, Charlie?"

Charlie finally turned to me, his face in shadows. "What about my mom, Faye?"

"What about her?" I was missing something crucial, but my head was a cobweb of panic. "I don't understand what you're asking."

"But if we—if we—*don't*," Charlie said, his voice a ragged whisper, "will her cancer come back?"

"Charlie is your *son*." My words were hard edges, chiseled from stone. "*Our* son."

"She's my mother."

"I won't give up Jonas."

"I understand how you feel." My mother's voice was soft, and full of compassion, but this just angered me more. But how could she understand? She went through with the sacrifice. She gave up my sister. I could not imagine the circumstances that would ever lead to me agreeing to such a proposition.

"She was your *daughter*." My voice was a low snarl, pregnant with venom.

"This is the responsibility—the *privilege*—of the town stewards," my mother continued as though I hadn't spoken. "It is our gift to the town. It's what makes our town special."

"Privilege?" I spat out the word. Disgust curdled like sour milk in my belly. "*Gift*?"

I'd always known I was next in line to be town steward, but I had never grasped the true price of that responsibility.

"Remember, Faye," my mother said, lips thinning. "You didn't even want to become a mother."

52

CHAPTER ELEVEN
PRESENT

JONAS IS NOWHERE in sight and panic comes in strobe-like jolts.

Jarring, physical bursts of sensation.

You never know how you might feel in a situation like this, what your body might experience if you were to wake up and discover that your baby wasn't where he was supposed to be. You don't realize that what you feel would be physical, that it would be deeper and more primal than fear.

Adrenaline pumps so fiercely and with such urgency through my veins I might black out.

I need to get it together.

Oh, god, where is he?

I can't think clearly.

Where is my baby?

I want to crumple on the forest floor, surrender to these elements, wither, decay and decompose like the fallen leaves and rotted moss.

No.

No.

I grit my teeth.

I have to find my baby.

I have to *find* him.

It's not over. We haven't come all this way, gone through all this for it to just be over.

53

And, just like that, my adrenaline fuels my actions.

I run out of the brush, our secret cave in the bushes. Where do I start? How would I *know* where to start? Oh, god. *Jonas.* I try not to think of wild animals, sneaking into our nest and stealing him away. Why him, and why not me? He is smaller. He is helpless. He is easier prey.

Oh, sweet Jonas.

I whirl around in the golden sunlight, another mockery. It is too happy, too laughing. The leaves rustle in the morning breeze. Everything is calm. There are no clues, or signs. The backs of my eyes burn. My chest prickles with heat.

I scream his name, despite wanting to stay hidden. I am desperate. My instinct has taken on a new shade of urgency. If anyone from town is close by, they will hear me. But that doesn't matter right now. What matters is finding Jonas.

Unless.

Unless.

I don't want to think it, but I can't help myself. What if he is dead, or worse? What if his body is mangled, torn to shreds by a wild animal. A bear? A wolf? A fox? A cougar?

Oh, my baby.

"Where are you?" My voice is raw, desperate. There are no tracks in the earth, no crushed leaves to indicate a path. There is only the abhorrent cheerful singing of the birds, the sound of the gentle breeze, the creaking of the tree branches, the rich smell of earth.

"*Jonas!*"

I am about to crumple, about to fall to the ground. About to collapse with dizzying despair. I am paralyzed with indecision, standing just outside our makeshift shelter. I had thought we were safe. I had tried so hard to keep us safe. And what did it matter? Something (*someone?*) still got my baby. I am afraid to move, afraid to take a step in the wrong direction because it is time I won't be able to make up. Time I won't ever get back.

The Forest

I squeeze my eyes shut and the tears are coming now, hot and panicked.

And then I hear it.

A sweet, soft babble.

His sweet, soft babble.

Jonas.

He's alive.

And his voice is carried on the breeze from somewhere to my right.

I run into the trees, thrash my way through a thicket.

I don't see him, but I can still hear him, still hear those sweet incoherent babbles. Oh, my baby.

My heart ricochets from my ribcage and my belly swells with nausea—a hangover from the adrenaline burst. But I am alive. Jonas is alive.

I round a small patch of trees and suddenly, I am in a clearing, and there he is, at the center of it.

Alone. Safe.

He is on his hands and knees, and he looks back at me and smiles broadly, his one front tooth sticking out.

I clasp my hands over my face. I can't help the burst of laughter that erupts from my core. "Oh, baby, look at you!"

My fear is forgotten, my panic dissipates. Because Jonas is *crawling*.

"What did you learn, big boy?"

I rush to him, scoop him up into my arms, my heart bursting with pride. I forget for a moment that we are on the run, that we are in hiding. Because in this moment, my baby boy has learned something new.

I think of Charlie, and I wish he were here with us to witness this, and my chest swells with sorrow.

"You gave Mommy quite a scare," I whisper. I kiss Jonas' cheek, then add, "Your daddy would love to see this." Because, in some universe, it's true, and Jonas can't understand what's happening. I don't need to burden him with a truth he can't even understand.

We need to eat breakfast and pack up for our day.

I carry Jonas back to our shelter and I am swept up in a dark sense of loss. It is in these moments, these moments of Jonas' first accomplishment, that I know I will miss Charlie the most. Charlie has betrayed us, I know that. I have done what is best for me and my son. But my heart hasn't caught up with my mind. I still remember the days before these awful truths came to light. I remember the way Charlie's curly black hair fell across his eyes just so. I remember his thick black eyelashes. I remember the way he smelled, like deodorant and soap and fresh cut grass. I remember the way he was with me when Jonas was born, not just there but *with* me, *with us.*

And right now, it hurts. I am heartbroken. I want my husband back, I want my family back, I want to go back.

And yet, I don't. I can't. We can't.

We can never go back to a reality that was just an illusion. But it was so beautiful while it lasted. So perfect while it was real, wasn't it? Wasn't it real, for a little while?

I press my cheek to Jonas' and he protests at the tight squeeze. I breathe in the milky smell of him. This is real. Jonas is real. And we are doing the right thing.

"Don't ever scare Mommy like that again, you hear me?" I murmur into his fuzzy ear. "Don't ever—"

I stop talking. I stop walking, stop moving, pray to the trees and sky that Jonas won't cry in this moment.

Because I hear voices. Footsteps.

Footsteps and voices.

Some of those voices are more immediately distinguishable than the others.

Charlie's. My father's.

And they aren't far away.

CHAPTER TWELVE
BEFORE THE FOREST

MY MOTHER'S WORDS were true. I *had* been uncertain about motherhood.

But her accusation, and the implication beneath it, hit me like ice water and took my breath away. It's as though she had pulled me inside out, exposed the soft vulnerability of my interior.

The birth control had been a sore spot between my mother and me. It was the most devastating fight we've ever had. No one but Charlie and his mother knew I was taking it. He'd wanted children, but we were still young. We *both* needed to be ready. Claudia had helped me order the contraceptives online, same as she did later when I needed sleeping pills. For all my parents' open mindedness it was the one outdated conviction my parents held: children were *always* a blessing, and nature should be invited to run its course.

Charlie and I kept our secret.

Only I'd slipped up one day and I had left my purse wide open and the tell-tale shell-shaped compact had been visible, and my mother had seen it.

She'd lost her typical composure, had gone ballistic. I'd never seen her react that way to *anything* and I'd been utterly baffled. And ashamed. Despite my modern sensibilities and Charlie's mother's reassurance that it was normal to want to wait, ingrained upbringing is a difficult thing to untangle. Charlie and I were happy—in love—and we'd told my parents we were trying. What was wrong with me that I couldn't get it together enough to let go, to give in *completely* to my life in Edgewood, to let go of my dreams even though everything had changed when I met Charlie? Deep down, I still wanted to leave and see the world. Charlie never would.

And I had chosen him, chosen *this* life, except . . .

Except.

There'd been a part of me that thought, *maybe*. Maybe, one day . . . and if we had a baby, that would all be over. We would be stuck in Edgewood. Trapped forever.

I stopped taking the birth control after my fight with my mother. I told Charlie I was ready, despite my doubts. He'd been so ecstatic and certain it nearly broke my heart. We became pregnant almost immediately.

I pressed my lips to the top of Jonas' soft head, felt the soft soothing pull of his suckle. "It doesn't matter, what I wanted before," I said. "He's here now. I wouldn't change it. I *won't*."

"This isn't easy for any of us." My father had been so silent that I'd nearly forgotten he was there.

His voice was a jolt of lightning, a shock that breathed light into his presence and cracked open the wall that had been holding back my emotions. My face was hot with betrayal. I began to cry.

"How can you ask this of me?" I whispered.

"We have to look at this objectively." His voice was low, far away. "Distance ourselves."

"Is that what you did? 'Distance yourself?' When you abandoned Autumn?"

"You make it sound as though what we did was selfish," my mother said. "When it's the opposite. It's the ultimate act of love. Of selflessness."

I shook my head. "I won't do it. We'll leave if we have

to. Forgo being town stewards. Live"—I waved my hand in a gesture meant to invoke the rest of the world, though the very thought filled me with terror—"out there."

"Babe." It was Charlie, anguished. "I'm staying here."

"Fine," I said. "But Jonas and I *aren't*, if it means—if it means—"

I couldn't bring myself to say the words, let alone believe them. Jonas nursed contentedly and I pulled him closer, drew strength from our physical connection the way his body drew nourishment from mine.

"Listen," my father said. "What's happening in our town? Bobby's *chickens*? Something is wrong. These things shouldn't be possible. We're concerned, that, well—"

"We think it has to do with how long you waited," my mother said.

"We never knew not to wait," Charlie said.

My mother brought her mug to her lips and paused, speaking over the rim. "Faye knew."

"I knew the birth control upset you," I said. "I didn't know *why*. You never told me. If you had—"

"If I had, then what?" My mother's words were razor sharp. "Would you have done it?"

I didn't reply, but I knew my face said enough.

My mother nodded. "Precisely. We couldn't risk it. The stewards have a responsibility to this town. It has always been the way."

"So, because we waited, Edgewood is, what?" I said. "Failing?"

"The shield that protects Edgewood," my mother said, "is finite. It only lasts so long. But because there was so much time between the last sacrifice and the next—"

"And by sacrifice, you mean Autumn." Now it was my turn to cut.

"Because there was such a big gap between offerings," my mother continued as though she hadn't even heard me, "the magic is wearing thin. It is breaking down. We must make the sacrifice at the Equinox, or things will only get worse.

"I don't care. I won't do it."

"Do you want to keep Edgewood safe?"

"Not like this." I ran my finger across Jonas' full, pink cheek. "It isn't right."

My mother reached across the table. "You mustn't forget." She placed her hand gently on my arm where Jonas' soft head was cradled into the crook of my elbow. "You have enjoyed the fruits of our sacrifice."

Her words stabbed a fresh wound through my heart, because she was right. I was complicit. My safety, my son's safety, in exchange for her life. The same safety I had clung to and relied upon ever since Jonas was born.

"I didn't know," I said, as if not knowing could ever be absolution enough.

My mother sighed, an exasperated sound, like I was the one missing something crucial. "Does that make you innocent? Faye, listen. Out there? The earth takes its sacrifices randomly—with no rhyme or reason, no order. In Edgewood, we have established a symbiotic relationship with nature, an agreement. We make a meaningful, deliberate sacrifice—made all the more powerful because it is a *willing* gift of that which is closest to our hearts—and the land complies. It protects us in exchange. It is that simple—and that specific. Anything less will throw our entire existence into chaos. We'll be no different than the world outside, no better. No safer. Everything we have worked for—everything we have already given—will be for nothing."

"Maybe you should have thought about that before giving up your daughter," I said. "You didn't have to do it, and neither do I. You have to reckon with your sins regardless of my choice."

"You're a fool to think you have one." My mother's lips were drawn tightly. "It is expected."

"By who?" My mother may have been a fine baker, but she'd taught me everything she knew. "Who else knows?"

"This is a steward secret, carried and protected by our lineage."

"Everyone should know," I said. "We benefit from the spoils of this shame. We are all already a part of this, whether we like it or not."

Dad shook his head. "It isn't their burden."

"This is *everyone's* burden."

My mother balked. "It isn't how things are done."

Charlie placed a hand on my shoulder, and I barely stifled a flinch.

"We'll take the day to consider," Charlie said. "Give us that?"

Just days ago, as recently as last night, the biggest worry in our town had been the mutilation of Bobby Perkins' chickens.

I changed Jonas to my other breast and smoothed my hand over the peach-fuzz at the nape of his neck. We craved safety here, we valued life. I wanted to believe that no one would sentence my son to certain death. That no one would ask that of me, no matter what may or may not be the consequences. But a voice from the dark recesses of my consciousness whispered wicked certainties. If my own husband—*my son's own father*—was uncertain, hesitant, how much more unlikely were the townspeople to side with us? To offer up their own valued and sacred safety, the birthright of everyone in Edgewood, for the spared life of a single child?

I nodded to show my agreement with Charlie. We would take the day if it bought me time to plan—though in my mind, there was nothing to consider.

My mother turned now to my father. "Eddie?"

Dad gazed at his hands, still wound tightly together on the worn wooden tabletop—the same tabletop that had seen so many family meals, heard so many tales of our day-to-day struggles, victories, and anecdotes, echoed with shared tears and laughter. That it was the hub of our family felt like an abomination, this one conversation sullying the wood to the point that no amount of staining could erase.

Dad's lips tightened, and it was how I knew he was deep in thought. I wished that his pale, thoughtful eyes would meet mine then, so that I might read his mind. We'd always shared a connection. I wanted him to look at me, but I was also afraid of what I might comprehend behind his eyes. That my kind, gentle father could wish me to do such an impossible thing—that he could have once given up his firstborn daughter to the whims and ravages of the dark forest—these incompatible ideas knocked together inside me, caused my insides to churn.

"It's a lot to take in," Dad said, finally. "You had your whole life, Lois. A day to process is more than reasonable."

Mom's finger worried at a knot in the wood on the tabletop. That her anxiety showed so freely disturbed me. My mother usually wore her confidence like the string of pearls around her neck. "A day won't make a difference. There is only one acceptable choice."

"Then give them space to grieve." My father's voice was low, baritone with the reverberations of finality. It was not a voice he used often, which made it all the more recognizable to us on the occasions when we heard it. In that moment, I suspected in him a possible ally, but I couldn't be certain.

"Fine." My mother's lips were tight, but even she knew when an argument with my father was futile. "A day to *process*."

We walked toward home in the translucent twilight, with Jonas strapped to my chest in the baby carrier. Charlie and I didn't speak. He was my husband, and yet, I did not trust him.

My thoughts were a tangled mess, cycling through my parents' words and Arrow's suspicious glances. Who was there to trust? I remembered Blossom's warm hand on my arm and softened some.

I reached for Charlie. "I need Blossom."

Charlie hesitated. "Shouldn't we get Jonas home?"

Jonas' body was warm against my own, and I looked down at him. "We do. But this is important."

"Okay. Give her a call when we get home, invite her over?"

I chewed my lip. I wanted to see Blossom right then, and her cottage at the edge of my parents' property was so close. But we did need to get Jonas to bed, keep him to his schedule. My body felt exhausted, the burden of staying upright a crushing weight. I longed for home, as if such a place still existed. "Yeah. Fine."

I kept my distance from Charlie as we walked, careful not to brush my arm against him the way I usually did. He must have noticed, because he reached for me. His hand was firm on my shoulder. He pulled slightly, enough that I stopped walking. Still, I couldn't bring myself to look at him.

"Faye." His voice was rough and low.

"Don't." My voice was barely a whisper. Any louder and it would crack.

"Please."

"What?" I said. My vision shimmered with tears.

"Talk to me."

"What is there to talk about?"

"You feel far away. I just want to know you're close. We're in this together."

"Are we?"

"I'm right here."

I shook my head. I'd reached an unbearable level of mental exhaustion from the day's trauma and I had no energy left. There was only one thing I wanted to hear Charlie say, and he refused to say it. And I didn't have the energy to explain why it was unacceptable. I shouldn't have had to explain.

I turned away from Charlie and continued walking. He hesitated at first, then reluctantly followed. Part of me felt guilty for refusing to connect, but I reminded myself that this was Charlie's own fault.

Anxiety swelled and roiled in my chest. I was going to have to leave. My parents wouldn't accept my refusal of the town's bargain and I couldn't trust Charlie not to give me away.

No. It had to be me and Jonas. It had to be soon. And it had to be a secret.

My mind reeled and I felt I might vomit from disorientation. My entire world had collapsed overnight, and my sanity was threatening to follow it.

I didn't *want* to leave Edgewood. I didn't want Edgewood to change. Our town was special. *Safe*. That was the promise, had always been. It's the only place I knew for sure that Jonas was protected.

(Except, *except*.)

This new dark knowledge clanged a discordant note in my mind, running up hard against what I had always known and accepted to be true.

Nothing bad ever happened here.

Except that wasn't true, was it?

It had never been true.

Without Jonas, the safety of this town was meaningless. If I didn't give Jonas up, the town would no longer be safe.

Was I being selfish?

Was it really my son's life, or everyone else's?

People always talked about the experience of unapparelled love after becoming a parent, that it was deeper and truer than any other love they'd ever felt. And it was true.

But they didn't tell you that a love this pure, a love this wonderful, would also consume you, fill you so completely, you choke.

The Forest

Because the love I felt for my child was *so* deep, *so* true, so *complete*, that it came with the potential to devastate a person.

If I lost him, I would unravel. To love someone so fiercely felt reckless. There was no bottom to what I would do to protect him. My love for Jonas was a precipice, the worst kind of height because of how far I could fall. It was a gaping, glaring abyss, dark and deep and black and always threatening, always tainting the edges of my joy.

Edgewood was my home. I wanted my son to grow up there, to spend his days in the forest, among the trees and foxes and squirrels and deer. I wanted him to grow up a little forest creature, just like I was.

But none of that mattered now.

It was too steep a price. Selfish or not, it was more than I was willing to pay.

CHAPTER THIRTEEN
PRESENT

THE VOICES OF my pursuers echo through the trees.

I clutch Jonas to my chest, and for a moment I am frozen with terror. I consider running from here, but we will be hopeless in these woods without our supplies. We won't survive a cool night without the protection of our blankets, and I need my water, and food. Our shelter from last night is, thankfully, in the opposite direction of where the voices are coming from. Moving as quietly as I possibly can, I hurry back to our campsite.

Once inside our bramble shelter, I tuck Jonas in the far end, the opening blocked, and give him a pacifier to keep him quiet. I consider hiding here until the voices pass. I debate this while I hurriedly pack our things.

The sounds play tricks on me. Sound is tricky, in a forest, with so many things to channel and redirect it. At times it sounds like they are closer; in other moments, it sounds like they're moving farther away.

I decide not to risk staying and hiding. We need to move. At this moment, I have the benefit of having some notion of their location, as well as a guess about the general direction in which they're headed. But there's no way to know how many of them there are, and it's unlikely that they are walking in a cluster. I assume they are spread out,

66

covering as much ground as possible to improve their chances of finding us.

My heart races as I strap Jonas to my chest. I hate that it's daylight. I wish it were night, so I could hide in the shadows, move through the forest's dark pockets.

But the golden light of sunrise has settled into the bright, unforgiving light of day, and wishing is a futile waste of precious time and energy.

I pull the backpack over my shoulders. I feel so weighed down with Jonas and the pack, but my rush of adrenaline gives me the strength to move quickly and stealthily.

I am, after all, a creature of the forest. The forest's betrayal doesn't alter the fact that I have grown up in these woods. I know them and I have to believe that they know me.

Your spirit heard my anguish from the forest.

My mother's words come back to me now. It's foolish, I know, to believe the stories that she told me as a little girl. So many stories, all of them lies. To think I once believed that I had been a fairy once, believed this was why I felt so at ease in these woods.

I once believed everything my mother told me.

My eyes smart with tears and I brush them away. I can't afford to cry right now. I need to be focused. I give my head a little shake, hoping to clear it. As I walk, I lift my shirt and help Jonas find my breast. He hasn't nursed this morning, and I can't afford for him to get cranky, to cry and give our location away.

When we were kids, my siblings and I used to play a game. We had to move through the forest without making a sound. We would play this game for hours. Perfecting our movements, practicing our skills, until finally one of us would break. Snap a twig or crunch a leaf. When the silence was finally broken, we would collapse onto the forest floor and howl, releasing all that pent up tension from our concentration.

Those summer days come back to me now, and I am playing with my brothers. Don't be the first one to make a sound.

I can still hear Charlie, and maybe that's Arrow he's talking to now. Hearing Arrow's voice bothers me. Arrow was always the best at the game, the quietest, the stealthiest. It was very rarely Arrow who ended the game, broke the silence.

Why are they being so loud?

The thought worries me, nags at me.

I have the sudden feeling that I am walking into a trap. Still, I walk, careful to remain silent, moving steadily away from the voices. My senses are heightened, alert. Step carefully, I tell myself, don't let them—

I enter a clearing, and my father emerges from behind a tree.

CHAPTER FOURTEEN
BEFORE THE FOREST

BLOSSOM'S FACE MIRRORED what I felt inside. "They want you to *what*?"

This gave me a sharp burst of hope. I was *not* being selfish.

I nodded. "Unbelievable, right?"

Both of my siblings had come over. Jonas was in bed, asleep. Charlie was hiding out in our bedroom, and I hadn't pushed him to join us. I couldn't bear to look at him just then. I didn't particularly want Arrow there, either, but Blossom had insisted when she'd heard the urgency in my voice. She had always believed the best of people. I wanted to. I watched Arrow intently, but he didn't look up from the brown bottle of beer in his hand. He was drawing lines through the sweat on the bottle with his fingertips.

"Arrow?" I said.

He looked up at me, his gaze a low smolder. "What?"

"What do *you* think?"

He shrugged and went back to fingering his beer. "You had to know there was something more than 'throwing shit into a fire' protecting this town."

I stiffened. "Did you?"

He shrugged again. "Not exactly. Guess I just never really bought it. Seemed like something to make everyone feel better, so we all feel like we're playing a part. But, I mean, come on. You think *every single person* offers what's most precious?"

"I never really considered—"

"Of course not." Arrow scoffed. "Jonas' newborn outfit? Really?"

"It's sentimental." Even I could hear the defensive lilt of my voice.

"Well, sure, but—"

Blossom made an exasperated sound. "*Enough.* Faye. You're not doing it. The sacrifice, I mean." She shuddered, because by *sacrifice*, she meant Jonas.

I shrugged. I wasn't going through with it, but I didn't want Arrow to catch wind of my plan and ruin it, somehow.

"Why wouldn't you?" Arrow said.

I blinked. "I shouldn't even have to answer that."

Arrow rolled his eyes, gulped a swig of beer. "It should have been me."

"Excuse me?"

"You heard me."

"Don't be a coward."

"Alright, Faye, you want to do this?" Arrow snarled. "I should have been town steward. You've never wanted it. I always have. That should matter."

"Maybe so. I don't make the rules, and if I did, I'd happily give you the job."

"Why don't you?"

"Because that's not how it works."

"If you're so concerned about the rules," Arrow said, "then why don't you follow them?"

"You mean, give Jonas up. You don't understand. How can you? You're not a father. You know our parents *murdered* Autumn, right?"

Blossom breathed in sharply and looked at her hands in her lap.

"They didn't *murder* her," Arrow retorted. "Don't be so dramatic."

"They abandoned her to the forest," I said. "You're arguing semantics."

"It's noble," Arrow said, sitting up taller. "They're willing to do something no one else could for the good of the whole. It's a true selfless act."

"Now you sound just like them. I should get the authorities involved."

"Sheriff Wilson?" Blossom said.

Arrow scoffed. "He's loyal to Mom and Dad. He'd never turn."

"Not Sheriff Wilson," I said. "Beyond him. Beyond here. This can't be legal."

"Of course it's not *legal*. This is Edgewood. We live by our own law."

Blossom gripped my hand. It was soft and warm in mine, which were frozen and papery. "I'm with you," she whispered.

Arrow rolled his eyes, but he didn't say anything. I squeezed her hand.

"What does Charlie think?" she said, her voice lowered.

I swallowed, a difficult feat. I glanced toward the direction of our bedroom down the hall and when I finally spoke, my voice was also hushed. "He's worried about his mom."

"Oh." A dark shadow of understanding bloomed on Blossom's face. "Oh, Faye. I'm so sorry."

I shrugged. "I don't think—I mean he hasn't exactly *said* . . . " It was too painful to say out loud. "He doesn't want her to get sick again."

"I am sure it was horrible for him." She spoke as though we were the only two in the room—and at that moment, we were the only two I cared about. I wished Arrow hadn't come. I didn't want to trust him with this terrible knowledge.

"It was," I said. "But losing Jonas is worse."

She nodded, her expression thoughtful. "You should tell everyone. The whole town. At the festival."

I shook my head, jaw set. "No. Absolutely not."

"He's *your* child," Blossom said. "They can't force you to do anything."

"They can't force me, but . . . " I chewed the inside of my cheek. "This bargain is what makes Edgewood . . . *Edgewood*. Do you think they'll give that up so easily? For one child?"

"But he's a *child*. An infant. It goes against everything Edgewood stands for."

"It does." I nodded. "Until it's between my child or theirs. Who do you think they'll choose?"

"It's not like every child in Edgewood will immediately drop dead if you don't do it." Blossom shook her head. "They've known you their whole life. Edgewood is built on a foundation of no harm."

Blossom cared, and I admired her urgency, but she wasn't a parent. She didn't understand the way dark thoughts can plague you, how safety was everything. I wondered if everyone in Edgewood was filled with secret fears, as I was. Maybe I wasn't an anomaly. Regardless: "It's also built on a foundation of sacrificed babies."

"Would you do it?" Arrow's voice was sudden and abrasive.

"What?" I said.

"Give up Jonas' guaranteed safety."

"Of course not. That's the point of this whole conversation."

"Not the sacrifice. But if it were someone else's burden?"

My face flared with heat and at first, I didn't have a reply. If the forest wanted someone *else's* child, *would* I go along with it to guarantee Jonas' safety? I shook my head, despite the shameful whispers that taunted me from the abyss. "They're *babies*."

"I don't think you have what it takes," Arrow said.

"Takes for *what*?" I really was sorry he was there.

"To be town steward," Arrow said. "Like it or not, it's your duty."

"My duty? My *duty* is to my child. I am Jonas' mother. I'm supposed to protect him."

"Yeah, and it sucks." Arrow stopped looking at me, the subtle pink of shame coloring his cheeks. Could his cold exterior have been covering something softer, more wounded? "But this is *Edgewood*. It will be—horrible—for you, I know. But Mom and Dad did it—for us, for everyone. And all the stewards before them. It's part of your responsibility, your burden. Without it, Edgewood's no better than any other place."

"And with it, we're worse."

Arrow didn't reply, but the intensity of his eyes, the certainty of his righteousness, didn't waver.

"Faye's right," Blossom said. Her cheeks were pink too, but with anger. "This pact sullies everything that's made Edgewood special."

"I know I sound cold," Arrow said. "But I'd do it. If it were me."

"But it's not you," I said. "It never will be."

"It should have been. I could do it. I *would*."

"An easy thing to say, another to actually do. You don't have children."

"Charlie's willing, you said it yourself."

"I didn't say he was *willing*. He's worried about his mom. That's different."

"How?"

The words hung in the air between us and it took everything in me not to scream that I was leaving, I was taking Jonas far away from here. Even out there in the harsh real world, where who knew *what* could happen, we'd at least have a fighting chance. Out there, I could fight for his safety. Here, we were trapped by tradition, expectations, customs.

Blossom squeezed my arm. "Wait a minute." Her voice was low and soft and soothing.

"There has to be another option."

"I won't do it," I said.

"Of course not," Blossom said. She paused, expression thoughtful. "What if you put it to a vote?"

I shook my head. "My son's life isn't up for debate."

"No," Blossom said. "But maybe you just say it is. Tell all of them, the whole town, at the festival."

"For what purpose?"

Blossom shrugged. "The truth, Faye." She gave Arrow a dirty look. "*Most* people would be appalled at the notion. Especially here. This changes *everything*."

"I don't know." I thought of my own fierce desire to protect Jonas, the lengths I'd go to save him. "People in Edgewood are attached to their comforts. We live here *because* it's special."

"They're good people," Blossom said. "You know them."

"They'll be afraid."

"They won't ask you to do this."

"How can you be sure?"

"Because it's Edgewood," Blossom said, simply. "You said it yourself: we're special. You grew up here. Everyone knows you. They won't ask you to make this sacrifice."

"I wouldn't be so sure," Arrow said. For once, I agreed with him.

"That's because you're a pessimist," Blossom retorted. She turned back to me, earnest. "Tell them what you're expected to do, and how you feel about it. Tell them you felt they deserved to know. Then put it to a vote."

"And if they vote in favor?"

"They won't."

"But if they *do*?" I said. "We're in an even bigger mess. And that's saying something."

Blossom squeezed my arm. "I'm *with* you, sister. I'd never let this happen."

"I know. And I appreciate it, I do. But it's too big a risk."

Blossom's forehead creased. "Well, what will you do then?"

I glanced at Arrow. "I don't know."

"You're underestimating them," Blossom said.

I shrugged. "Maybe. Even so, it's no one's decision but mine."

"And Charlie's," Arrow cut in.

I looked at him, my gaze steady. "Yes. And Charlie's."

CHAPTER FIFTEEN
PRESENT

MY FATHER TAKES one step toward me. It takes every ounce of my willpower not to scream.

Instead, I step back.

He places a finger to his lips.

I cock my head, curious now, uncertain.

His body is rigid, tight with the urgency that radiates off of him in waves. His finger is still pressed, almost violently, to his lips, mashing them. His eyes are still connected with mine. He is trying to tell me something. He shakes his head once.

He points in the direction of the voices, and shakes his head again.

He points in the direction I was headed. Another shake of the head.

I *was* walking into a trap. This is what he's trying to tell me.

But how can I trust him?

He points in a third direction now, and this time he nods.

I knit my eyebrows together. I am trying to ask him: *How can I trust you?* But I don't dare speak.

He places his hand to his heart. *I'm so sorry*, he mouths. Then he points at me. At us. *I love you. I love Jonas.*

THE FOREST

I think of the way my father wouldn't look at me on that first day, when we sat at their worn wooden dining table.

Why?

My father shakes his head, more urgently now, and points in that third direction again. *Go. Now.*

He steps toward us, and I step back, and his shoulders slump. His eyes meet mine, beseeching, and he is honest with me in this moment. I know it. I feel it. I can trust him. I have no other choice.

He wraps his arms around me. I breathe in the familiar scent of him, a smell I've known so long I can't even describe it. It's just the smell of my dad. The smell of home.

There's no place like home.

I return the embrace.

It's short. My dad grabs me by the shoulders, holds me at arm's length. He mouths, *I'm sorry*, again. He kisses the top of Jonas' head. Then points in that third direction. *Go. Quick.*

And we do.

CHAPTER SIXTEEN
BEFORE THE FOREST

WHEN I **WOKE** the next morning, I experienced the cruelest of betrayals: the amnesiac effect of sleep, the promise of the day's first light. Jonas' coos drifted down the hallway into our bedroom, sweet as honeysuckle perfume on the breeze. I smiled in that moment, which felt as perfect as any ordinary morning: my favorite time with Jonas.

But the thought of him brought the moment to a violent halt, sent my heart into my throat.

It all rushed back in one bitter instant, and the morning light seemed suddenly harsh and impatient.

I closed my eyes and wished for sleep, wished to return to that place of numb bliss, wished to forget again. Or better, to turn back time.

Jonas' cries became more insistent.

I stepped lightly out of bed, tiptoed from the bedroom. I didn't want to wake Charlie. I was always amazed at his ability to sleep soundly through all of Jonas' noises, while I stirred with even the most minor of sounds. Jonas' delicious babbling nonsense filled the hall, echoed off the walls like those soft whispers of morning light. How cruel those small beauties felt that day.

I tightened my robe around myself, feeling exposed

and vulnerable in my own home. Even the walls seemed ominous, with their potential to become my prison.

When I reached his room, Jonas' face erupted into a smile. He grasped his toes and beamed up at me from between the wooden bars of his crib. I gathered him into my arms, pressed my face into the nape of his soft neck, breathed in his milk-sweet scent. I carried him back down the hall, into our bed. We curled up together beneath the white cotton sheets and I lay on my side, lifted my shirt so he could nurse. He latched onto me and nuzzled against my skin, his lashes soft and golden brown in the cool haze of morning light. I hadn't known anything could be so beautiful.

We lay like that, our bodies cocooned together, and the world went soft and dreamlike around the edges.

Charlie slept still, his gentle snores mingled with Jonas' rhythmic swallows to create our morning song. The sweetness of the moment made the edges of the ache inside me more acute and defined.

In that whispery light I could almost pretend that I wasn't angry with Charlie. But worse than that: hurt, betrayed.

In the honeyed light of morning, I could almost pretend nothing had changed. But it had. The foundation of trust we'd built our relationship on was crumbling, so quickly I could hardly bear it.

I turned my attention back to Jonas, because thinking of Charlie was like prodding a bruise.

This was our daily ritual. I savored the bittersweet taste of those quiet mornings. Each one meant one day less with Jonas, one day less he was my baby.

I didn't want my thoughts to creep back into those dark places.

No.

I closed my eyes against the stab of anxiety that cut into my belly, swallowed the acrid taste of bile that rose with my fear.

This love was wonderful and I could not bear to lose it.

The sleeping pills had helped temper the dark edges of my thoughts, but today my fears were real. I stood on the precipice of total annihilation. The abyss was hungry, and as ever, it loomed.

I was suddenly questioning the things I once held as absolute truths: that our town was safe. That Edgewood loved me as much as I loved it. That my parents would do anything to protect their children. That nothing bad could ever happen in the forest.

The autumn equinox was three days from now, when Charlie and I were to become town stewards. The fall festival began that morning. The festival happened every year, but the ceremony only occurred when there was a new town steward. There hadn't been a ceremony since when my parents were initiated. I had been so looking forward to the event, so steeped in the aura of history and legend.

The thought of it now brought a sour taste to the base of my tongue.

Of course, none of it was going to happen. Jonas and I would not be here.

I looked down at my infant then, his eyes closed, eyelashes soft against his full, pink cheeks. I traced the soft fuzz along the rim of his ear. What would I do to protect him?

The answer was simple. I already knew what I would do.

Anything that was necessary. Anything at all.

CHAPTER SEVENTEEN
PRESENT

MY **FATHER HAS** given us some time but that doesn't mean we have much of it. They could still overtake us, collide with us; our paths could still intersect despite all of my father's good intentions.

My father.

His help seemed genuine. His eyes. I don't doubt his sincerity. How can I? I have no other choice. He could have sent me right into a trap. But why would he bother doing that? Why not just grab us when he had the chance, when we were right there in front of him?

Unless he wanted me to believe that he was helping.

No.

I won't let myself believe that.

While the last few days have proven only that I don't know what is true anymore, what is real, who I can believe—I do know that I have felt my father's love. I have felt it, real and full and all-consuming, my entire life. He loves me. He loves Jonas. He *does*.

I wonder if he's ever been comfortable with these traditions? Perhaps he never wished to go along with it. But my mother—well, she is my mother. She is strong and fierce and wise—or so I once believed—and she has her ways of convincing. There is no way to view the world but through her eyes. I wonder if my father sees it. I wonder if this is his way of standing up, of fighting back.

I feel the strain of the backpack, and of Jonas on my front, yes—but I feel more than that. I feel anger. I press my hand firmly against Jonas' back.

Why hasn't my father fought before?

Why has he gone along with something so clearly evil?

How did he let her get away with it?

How could he abandon Autumn?

How could he let my mother force this terrible curse onto me, onto *us*?

Whatever happens to us—whatever the outcome—my conscious is clear. I am doing what I know is right. I am giving it my all. And if they catch us—if they force this fate onto me, onto Jonas—that blood, that darkness, that evil is on their hands.

Not mine.

But I will fight.

I want to feel grateful for the mercy my father has just shown us, but instead I am seething. It's not enough. It's too late. And it's cowardly, a thing he's doing in secret. Why couldn't he stand up for us before? Why couldn't he have helped protect us? He could have—

But I'm not paying close enough attention to where I'm walking, and I lurch suddenly forward. My foot is swallowed by the earth. Too late, I realize there's a sinkhole, hidden by the covering of leaves on the forest floor. It takes all my will to avoid crying out, and desperately, I wrench my body so I don't land on Jonas.

It works. The backpack breaks my fall, somewhat, but it's still a jolt of a landing.

It shocks Jonas and he begins to cry.

His wail is fierce and slices into the crisp fall air, neatly and with precision.

"Shhhh," I hiss, with too much ferocity. I struggle to my feet. My ankle screams with cold white pain. I limp forward, and as I do, I fumble with the opening of my coat, my flannel shirt. Jonas is frantic now, tired of being carried, protesting against the constraints of the baby carrier. I don't blame him, but I can't think of his comfort now. This is about keeping him safe.

I offer him my breast, and he accepts it greedily, sucks too hard. The pull of his mouth stretches my skin taut. I flinch, but I don't care about the discomfort. What I need is his continued silence.

There is no path in this part of the forest. I don't have time to consult my compass. I don't know where the search party will be coming from, but I know that Jonas' cries have disclosed our location.

And then I hear them.

Footsteps.

Hushed and hurried voices. Constrained shouts and directives.

They are closing in on us.

Oh, Jonas, my poor, sweet boy.

I am irritated with him, but deeper down I am upset with myself. I should have been more careful, more focused. I should have watched my footing. I know better, I understand the deception of these forest floors.

Move.

Trying to hurry us away from those voices, those intimidating footsteps. The rush of the nearby river calls to me, a beacon of hope. With each step, I worry that I am moving in the wrong direction, that we will reach a dead end, a corner, a trap.

A sharp cramp throbs just below my ribcage. I should ditch the backpack, but I know we need the supplies. I keep moving, but the voices keep getting closer. They are trying to be quiet, but I can hear them—all of them. So many of them, and only two of us. We are running out of space, out of time.

I'm sorry, Jonas. I'm so sorry, my baby. Mommy tried. Mommy tried to save you.

The voices, the footsteps—all closer. All closing in on us. I am moving as fast as I can but I am just one person. Jonas suckles contentedly at my breast, unaware of the fate about to befall us. Unaware of the terrible things that await him.

I dare a look behind me and something flashes through the cracks in the trees. *Oh, god. Oh, Jonas.*

The surge of adrenaline has run out, and I am hitting a wall, I am burning out, I am crashing. I can't keep up this pace much longer. *You have to.* I can't. *You will. You must.*

The back of my neck prickles and I know they are closer. Perspiration stings my pores and I pant, panicked, as their shouts become urgent, their footsteps more distinct and certain.

This can only mean one thing: they have spotted me.

The speed of my footsteps feels supernaturally fueled. I didn't realize I was capable of moving so quickly. They may be upon us in mere moments, but I will not give up. The more energized they sound, the closer they get, the more determined I become. It's not over till it's over.

There is a massive tree up ahead.

I know I shouldn't stop, but I need to breathe.

I hide behind the tree, even if it is futile. We are too open, too exposed. My pulse is a living thing that throbs in my throat. They are too close.

I look down at the tree, and I notice that the hollow is large enough for a person to hide in. Maybe not a person with a baby and a backpack, but—

Then I see something inside, something strange.

I stick my head into the hollow for a closer look.

Something is in there.

I reach my hand inside the tree, and my fingers graze a rough and cool surface.

Cement?

There is a large, grey slab of cement inside the trunk of

the tree. It is hidden by the shadows so you can't see it unless you're as close as I am. Someone passing casually by would never notice.

I duck inside the tree. The space is just big enough for me to fit—baby carrier and backpack all—but only *just*. Jonas is momentarily scrunched and he whines quietly, then goes back to nursing.

I grip the cement slab with both of my hands, and pull.

Miraculously, the slab dislodges easily.

Even more miraculous is what's behind it. A deep, black tunnel that is submerged within the earth. Stairs sculpted from hard-packed earth lead down into that black place.

I heave the slab all the way to the side and step onto that earthen stairway.

I pull the cement slab back into place behind me.

The darkness is all-encompassing. I grip the walls and move carefully, descend down, down, down into the earth.

I don't know what this is, or who built this tunnel, or who it belongs to. All I know is that by some miracle, Jonas and I are safer than we were just moments ago.

At the bottom of the earthen stairs, I feel the momentary relief of reaching level ground. I reach an uncertain hand into the dark and my fingers connect with a wall of hard-packed soil. We are in some kind of underground tunnel, now.

I don't know where we are, or where it leads.

I can't be sure that no one else will find the tunnel and follow us down here. Still: for now, we are safe. I feel around and note that to my left, there is nothing but a dirt wall. The tunnel—wherever it leads—opens only to the right. I take a deep breath and step into the dark.

CHAPTER EIGHTEEN
BEFORE THE FOREST

I DIDN'T GREET Charlie when he finally woke up and joined us in the kitchen. He entered the room, saw Jonas in his high chair with chunks of cheddar cheese and fresh berries, me with a bowl of fruit and yogurt. Noticed the single cup of coffee on the table.

I knew he would realize there was not a second cup for him, nor a bowl of sliced fruit waiting for him as there usually was. Of course he would. That was the point.

He stood at the entryway to the kitchen, observed us silently. I watched him from the corner of my eye, but I wouldn't look at him directly.

He went straight to the cabinet, retrieved a bowl and a mug. He poured himself a cup of coffee, then joined me at the table.

"Babe," he said after a long moment.

"Don't." My voice was cold and sharp, like the knife smeared with fruit stains on the counter.

"Let's talk."

"About?" I squeezed my hand into a fist on the table, the accusation in my heart welling up into my eyes.

Charlie hesitated.

Disgust filled me and I did nothing to hide it. I wanted him to see it. "Unless you're sitting there to tell me that you love me and Jonas and you'll do everything in your power to protect him—unless you're going to tell me that you won't agree to this—this—*abominable* thing, I don't want to hear it."

"I do love you and Jonas," Charlie said. "But—"

"But?" My voice quavered. "How is there a 'but'? If you love me and Jonas, that's where it ends."

"What about my mom?"

"What *about* her?"

"Look, you didn't see how she was," Charlie said. The expression on his face was pained. "Before we came here."

I felt the slightest whisper of compassion for his perceived dilemma.

"We don't know that the cancer will come back."

"We don't know that it won't."

Jonas squealed, impatient for me to replenish the berries on his high chair tray. "Sorry, buddy," I cooed, and scraped more sliced pieces of strawberry in front of him. His mouth was smeared with red stains.

I returned my attention to Charlie. "But we don't *know*."

"I can't see her suffer—"

"No. It's wrong. This bargain ends here."

"But, Edgewood."

"Will be different. I know."

A fine line appeared between Charlie's thick black eyebrows. "But doesn't it make all the rest of it a waste? All the sacrifices that came before?" He paused. "What about your sister? Autumn?"

I flinched. Another truth that had turned the rosy filter of my childhood a distorted, sickly grey. "Their lives can never be replaced or redeemed. And that's tragic. It is. But just because mistakes were made in the past, doesn't mean we go on making them once we know better. That isn't how progress works."

"But Edgewood *is* progress." Charlie's voice was low and his eyes met mine, earnest.

"You can't mean that. Knowing what we know."

"You haven't lived, out there." Charlie's gaze intensified. "You don't know what it's like. How afraid people are. People get sick, people die, for no reason. It's no way to live, Faye. Edgewood is . . . there's no place like it. It's found a way around all that. Don't you think we should protect that?"

"At what cost? This *place* is supposed to be safe. For *everyone*." I pressed gently along my temple where a headache was building. "*You* don't understand, Charlie. You didn't grow up *here*."

Charlie's head snapped up. "It's precisely because I didn't grow up here that I *do* understand. My mother was sick before we came here. Sick, Faye. You don't know what that's like because *you can't*. She was nearly destroyed. We were out of hope—out of options—and then I got that anonymous email." I knew the story, but I let him tell it anyway. "It was crazy, Faye. For us to up and leave like that. Ludicrous, you know? To think she could be saved by a town. But—it worked, Faye. *It worked*. A week after we got here, she started to improve, and it all just—went away. How do you explain that?"

I couldn't explain it, of course. It was the way things were, there. And Charlie's story wasn't exceptional, not in Edgewood. There were two kinds of people in our town: those who grew up here, and those who found it when they needed it most. Edgewood was not a place that could be found if you went looking for it, unless it wanted you to find it. Unless it needed you.

I had a sudden and horrible suspicion that this town needed Charlie more than I'd ever understood. Because it needed me.

Because it wanted me to stay.

Thinking of it then, it seemed absurd that I had grown up with a peripheral acceptance of the notion that my town had a sentience of its own. That I had accepted this place as sacred, rather than an aberration.

Charlie was wrong. Edgewood was not special. It was no different from the world outside, the world that scarred Charlie so. It still took its sacrifices in blood, just like any other place. Only this was more insidious because we had agreed to its rules, succumbed to the forest's demands. What kind of benevolent being fed off the lives of innocent children?

Their deaths were not meaningless. They were not wasted. They had brought me here, and I had the power to stop the cycle. To honor them by refusing to allow this torrid legacy to continue.

I thought of the forest, and all the years I spent wandering carefree amongst its trees, and I shivered.

Jonas finished his breakfast. I used a wet wipe to clean the strawberry stains from his face and hands. He beamed up at me, his eyes large and deep brown, just like his father's. I lifted him from the chair and carried him into the living room. I placed him on the carpet in front of his toys. He grabbed a red wooden block with each hand, banged them together with unabashed glee.

Charlie sat down beside me and rubbed my shoulder. It was something he did to soothe me when I was anxious and my muscles softened in spite of myself. Could I have gotten through to him?

Perhaps this part of the nightmare was over, and my Charlie—the *real* Charlie—had returned. He leaned into me, pressed his warm, full lips to my ear, kissed gently. My body wanted to yield, wanted to believe in the power of the promises he'd made. My skin erupted into goose bumps, a not unpleasant sensation.

"We could have more children," he whispered.

I pulled away sharply. "None of them would be Jonas."

"Hear me out."

I shook my head. I didn't want to hear any of this. But Charlie continued.

"Look at your parents," he said. "Your family. You're all happy."

"We *were*."

"You are. And they've been through it. They'd know how to help us."

"I would never forgive myself."

"Your parents would do anything for you."

"Not *anything*," I said, because though I could hardly believe it myself, I had learned this to be true.

I thought of our years as a family, my memories of childhood that had always gleamed with golden light. That light had turned sickly and yellow. The memories of happiness ached, like lies.

"It would hurt for a while," Charlie continued, though his words were unbearable.

"It would hurt forever."

"Maybe," he said, and nodded. "It would be awful, to—to lose him, I admit it. The thought knots my stomach. But if it means—if it's for the greater good—"

"There is no greater good without Jonas," I said. "Just a single drop of poison spoils the pot." And this gave me an idea.

"We can have more children," he said again, absurdly. "We will love them too, just as much, maybe more, after everything. They would never have to know."

"Like I never had to know?" I said. "Until it's their turn to be town steward, and we pass along this terrible curse? This whole town and everyone in it, and the safety and the healing and the miracles, it's a curse, Charlie, a blight. It's not the blessed place we think it is, not with this—this *stain*." A sob escaped my lungs and it surprised me. "We're talking about children, Charlie. Children. Babies. *Our baby*." This last: barely a whisper.

I thought of Jonas, waiting in the dark forest, abandoned, crying out for me. What if his last memory was of that bewildered waiting, wondering where on earth his mother had gone, and why she had left him there? It hurt me just to *think* of it, to imagine his hopelessness—let alone what other horrors he might experience. I shook my head, tried to dislodge the image.

No.

No.

"And we would know," I said. "*We* would know." How could safety ever taste so sweet to anyone, once they knew what it had cost?

"He's so young, Faye. He wouldn't suffer long. He wouldn't even remember that he'd suffered."

That Charlie could think these words, let alone speak them, told me how far away from each other we truly were.

"It doesn't matter," I said. "It's simply not an option."

I joined Jonas on the floor and refused to continue the conversation.

CHAPTER NINETEEN
PRESENT

THE MILDEW STENCH of wet, decaying leaves and forest rot increases in strength down here in this tunnel. Like I'm moving closer to the source of the smell. Or like it's moving closer to me.

My fingers grope at the moist soil on the earthen walls as I feel my way through the length of the tunnel. My ankle still throbs from when I twisted it, but the pain has dulled to a warm ache. It is pitch dark in this tunnel—blacker than night, with no ambient light leaking in through any cracks. We are sealed in. Protected. (*Trapped!*) I crave the light from my flashlight. My fingers graze tangled roots, loosen small rocks.

The wet green smell of rotting earth and moss gets stronger.

I consider opening my bag, but a deep instinct warns me against using my flashlight right now. I already feel like we are being watched. Like there is something—*someone!*—down here with us in the dark. Something that's following me. Something—*someone!*—that's been following us this whole time.

Again, I think of the shelter, the way it also stank like wet earth within its makeshift walls. I remember the chicken bones, with bits of flesh and blood still clinging to them.

The Forest

What is it about being underground that breeds thoughts of skeletons and specters? Of burial? Of death?

I touch Jonas' cheek. He has drifted to sleep. He snores softly.

The inability to see has sharpened my senses. Perhaps this is why I notice the smells of a decaying forest. Maybe it's not that there is anything down here with us besides the hidden earth, and it's just that my senses are heightened to make up for my lack of sight. I breathe in, I breathe out. The smell is thicker, stronger.

Cloying.

(*Closer!*)

I try not to make a sound, but it's impossible to achieve silence when I am stumbling my way down here in the dark.

And then I hear it.

I freeze, wish I could pull Jonas even closer.

Blood thrums in my ears, so loudly I have to strain to listen for any other sounds outside of it.

But I do hear it again, a soft, creeping rustling sound. A large sound. It is trying to be quiet, and it is used to this dark tunnel, and so it moves quieter than me. But I can still hear it. Creeping. *Following.*

The green mildew stink gets thicker, riper, more robust.

Something *is* getting closer. *Someone.*

We are not alone in the tunnel.

I cup my hand around the side of Jonas' head, as though my soft flesh is enough to protect his vulnerable skull. I swallow, dryly, desperate, my ears straining. I want to move, but I am frozen with fear and the inability to comprehend what might be down here with us.

I want to go home.

There's no place like home.

There's *no place.*

My eyes swell with heat and moisture and I clench my

teeth to fight back tears. A war wages within me as my body debates between fight or flight. Don't move. Play dead. Be still. *Run*.

And then I am filled with a rush of anger. A sudden determined resolve. *Fight*. I stand up straighter in this endless dark, this deep black tunnel in a forest that wants to swallow us whole.

I will not let the forest have me. I will not let the forest have Jonas.

"Who's there?" My voice, harsh and sharp, vibrates into the dark.

Whatever—*whoever*—is following us stops.

I can hear it breathing.

I don't know how I didn't hear it before.

The sound is low, quiet, barely there. A strange, incongruous sound, a wild sound, like wind moving through trees or tiny creatures shuffling through dried leaves on the forest floor.

But it is there.

And it is close.

Something is close.

Someone is close.

My skin prickles with fear and rage and I am *tired*, but I won't go down without a fight.

With one hand, I cup the back of Jonas' head. With the other, I grip the wooden beads of my Rowan necklace.

"What do you want from me?"

That breathing again. Low. Soft. Rustling.

It is not a human sound.

The sharp green stink of forest rot is strong, but it stops moving closer. I can feel that, sense it. The thing has stopped. We stand there in our invisible face-off, me with my hot hand curved around Jonas' skull, the wooden beads moist in my sweating fingers, my lower lip set. The darkness swirls, dances with shapes that aren't there as my eyes strain to see through it, *into it*, to transcend and defy it.

The Forest

At first, it is subtle.

And then I am sure of it.

The smell has lessened. It isn't as strong as it was, moments ago.

The thing that waits for us in the dark is moving away.

And then the smell nearly fades all together. It is still there. A whisper. A memory. The faint suggestion that something—*someone*—had been here, had lingered, had breathed in the taste of our breath.

I can't hear the breathing anymore. Can't hair the soft, subtle scratching of footsteps in the dark.

And somehow I know we are safe, for now. There is something down here with us in the dark, but it has, for the moment, retreated.

This isn't as comforting as it should be, because I fear a reckoning is still to come.

The thing that lurks down here in the dark has backed away, given us our space. But it isn't *gone*, hasn't left us alone down here in the dark. It is still aware of us, can still smell us, taste us. It is still ripe and curious with need, with want. With hunger.

I understand that, feel it in my bones.

And, after all, we are not yet out of the woods.

THE LATE-AFTERNOON AIR was alive with golden sunlight and thick with the heavy aromas of firewood smoke, burnt caramel, and sizzling meats. Charlie and I walked toward the town square; Jonas was strapped to my chest in the baby carrier, facing out. He liked to watch everything when we walked, take the world in.

Charlie attempted to hold my hand but I shied away, could hardly believe he would even attempt to touch me. Next he reached for Jonas' soft, curly head and I balked, jumped sideways so we were out of his reach.

"Come on, Faye." Charlie's voice was low. We were nearly to the square. "Don't be like that."

"How should I be?"

"We're in public. You're still my wife. He's still my son."

I cupped my hand around Jonas' fuzzy ear. "Then act like it."

"It's not that simple."

"You should have taken your sleeping pills," Charlie muttered. His words pressed against a disagreement we'd had last night, still a fresh bruise.

"I already told you." I gritted my teeth. "I didn't want them." Those little white pills were so tempting, my mouth watered, yet I resisted the call of their false comfort.

THE FOREST

Anxiety had a purpose, in the right place and time. It was built into our bodies as a security system, an alarm that went off when something was wrong. I wanted all of my facilities fully functioning. No numbness, no false quiet.

Charlie's gait slowed, then he took large strides to catch up. "I just don't want everyone to see us and think something is wrong."

"Something *is* wrong, Charlie."

But he was partially right. I needed to play this better, mask my emotions. I didn't want anyone to suspect my true intentions.

We stepped onto the town square lawn, and Jonas pointed at the large bonfire at the center. "Yes, baby!" I said. "Fire!"

He squealed with delight and my heart squeezed. The festival was usually my favorite time of year, but tonight, my joy fell flat.

I eyed the piles of goods at the edge of the fire. Fruits and vegetables from local gardens, handmade rocking chairs, musical instruments, piles of folded clothing, trinkets, dolls, toy soldiers. Everyone in town—even the children—participated in this yearly expression of thanksgiving. This farce, as I now knew it to be.

Every year at the fall festival, we celebrated another year of prosperity and safety. We gathered to eat, drink, dance, laugh. The children dashed around the square, stayed up way too late and overfilled themselves with kettle corn and all manner of other fall treats. For a town as miraculous as ours, we were surprisingly devoid of organized religion and dogma. Even so, we were not without our rituals.

Each festival began with the citizens bringing goods to the great bonfire. There were no stipulations as to what the offering should be, beyond one very important thing: the chosen goods must matter to the individuals who offered them. Giving them up had to be a sacrifice.

The heart of the sacrifice was gratitude, and—I thought with burning shame—it was this act we had believed to have purchased and secured our safety. *Goods* in return for protection.

If only it had ever been that simple. A price paid in anything less than blood was not a price at all.

If I had been asked to articulate what we were giving thanks to, I probably would have said something about *the land*. If I had been asked to expound, I would have realized that what I really meant by that was *the forest*.

It had always been the forest.

Arrow was right. On some level, I had always known it. I had been so foolish, so willing to pretend.

The late-summer evening air felt suddenly thick and stifling.

What would these people do, if they learned the goods they had been tithing for years were not what the forest truly required? My pace slowed. I observed the wealth at the edge of the fire, the treasures the townspeople were willing to sacrifice to preserve their safety.

I placed my pointer fingers to the inside of Jonas' soft palms, and his fingers curled around them. The sensation grounded me. It wasn't as strong or unbreakable as the umbilical cord that once tethered us and bound our blood, but it was just as life-giving.

My family was gathered near the podium at the back edge of the square. Every muscle in my body tensed, ready to run, but still my feet carried me toward them. Blossom leaned forward to kiss Jonas' cheek and then mine. She squeezed my arm. "You okay?" she mouthed.

I nodded.

The sounds of the impending celebration around me were too much for my senses. Children laughed. The jovial voices of neighbors greeting one another carried on the breeze. For the first time, I heard the falseness in those too-sweet voices. The anxiety I had struggled to keep at bay crested. I craved silence and solitude. I wished for Jonas and me to be far away already.

I felt my mother's gaze, but I didn't return it. The only one I made eye contact with was Blossom: my reassuring anchor. I released one of my hands from Jonas' grip so I could reach for one of hers; it was soft and warm. Charlie touched the back of my neck, but I inched away from him. Jonas squirmed in the carrier.

My father lifted the black foam microphone to his lips. The speakers emitted a high-pitched squeal.

"Sorry about that." My father boomed from the speakers, a wave that sent ripples of calm through the celebratory crowd. His voice had that effect.

It even worked on me. I was confused and angry, but he was still my father. The love I felt for him in that moment was a wrench in the coils of my gut. His smile was full of sorrow and I couldn't bear it.

"Well, now," he continued. "We've made it through another year. Hard to believe the summer's already over. The fall festival is a special time—I know I look forward to it every year. Mrs. Barkley, I could smell your famous apple pies baking from a mile away."

Mrs. Barkley, a stout woman with a puff of white hair, beamed from the front of the gathered crowd. I noted soft lines of her pale face, the pearl earrings that pulled at the sagging skin of her earlobe. My back straightened and her kind eyes gave me confidence. Blossom was right. I had known these people my whole life. I grew up in this town. They were like family. They wouldn't ask me to do this terrible thing.

Even as the thought entered my mind, I was fighting against a worse one. *It's my own family asking me to do this terrible thing in the first place.* But no, that was wrong. Because it wasn't my *whole* family. I remembered Blossom's words and I clung to them.

"Now, to follow tradition, Arrow and I will light the

bonfire," Dad said. "And while we do, my lovely wife here is going to tell the story of Edgewood, as is tradition."

A story that was a lie, I thought bitterly.

Dad continued, "And as you well know, Faye will officially be assuming the duties of town steward in a few days, joined by Charlie in his sacred duty as steward's spouse. This is the last year Lois and I will be officiating the ceremony. It has been our pleasure and honor to serve this town all these years. That it's coming to an end is bittersweet, but I think you'll find our daughter and her husband here to be capable leaders."

The gathered crowd erupted into a cacophony of applause: whistles and cheers, clapping and yelps and howls and laughter. My father and Arrow began the process of lighting the fire, and my mother approached the microphone.

"Once upon a time," she began, as was tradition, "the world was in pain. There was hurting, and heartache, and disease, and tragedy. And our ancestors wandered into the forest. What they wanted was to create a place where they'd have their own rules, their own quiet, hidden way of life. They wandered in the forest for days, questioned their own sanity, their own vision—they nearly gave up faith, nearly turned back."

I swallowed. I could hardly bear to listen to her blasphemies. I struggled to slow my breathing, remembered that I needed to appear calm and collected. I had to let the façade continue, for just a little while longer.

"But their persistence was rewarded, as it so often is. Because they found, in the middle of the great woods, a clearing. And they soon discovered that this land was special. A well-kept secret meant just for them, hidden away for those who dared to seek for it. Those people were the first settlers of Edgewood, and since then, this has served as a haven. A beacon of light in a dark world. A place where harm can befall none. Where the people love each other, where the—"

THE FOREST

There was a commotion. It took me a moment to process what was happening, and by the time I did, Blossom had already gently—but firmly—pushed our mother away from the podium. The expression on her face was bright and beatific, and my belly swelled with dread.

"I'm sorry to interrupt our lovely tradition," Blossom said, and I shook my head. Her gaze passed slowly over the gathered crowd. "But there is something I need to address before we can proceed with the evening's festivities."

The crowd mumbled amongst themselves, a quiet rumble in the growing dark.

"I know that you all believe Edgewood is special. How can you not? We hear it our whole lives. Some of us—many of us—have experienced miracles. We know the joys of sleeping soundly, knowing our loved ones are safe in their beds. That they're protected by a force beyond ourselves. That comfort is so precious, so deeply ingrained into our way of life here. And I know all of you believe it is our yearly offerings that protects this town. I believed it myself until—until recently. But I—I have recently learned that it is something else. Something worse. Something—unthinkable."

This was my moment, my last chance to keep my carefully spun plan from unraveling. Blossom caught me approaching. I shook my head, my eyes wide and feral.

Please, I mouthed.

Blossom looked away quickly, and her next words tumbled from her in a rush.

"The truth is, the town stewards have ritually sacrificed their first-born children to the forest."

I froze.

A collective gasp escaped from the crowd.

The sound gave me a brief moment of hope. Was it possible Blossom was right? Had she saved us? I pulled Jonas closer in the carrier.

"Many of you will remember our sister, Autumn," Blossom said.

"She wandered too far into the forest," Mrs. Barkley said. "Got past the boundary."

The pervasive nature of the lie sickened me.

"No," Blossom said, her voice wavering slightly. "My parents gave her to the forest. Deliberately. Haven't any of you ever questioned it? Wondered how something so terrible could happen *here*?"

They didn't reply, but the crowd shuffled, and the guilty looks on the sea of faces confirmed that I had not been alone in my curiosity. But I realized something then, something worse about all of us: we were comfortable, happy, safe. We didn't want to look at this tragedy too closely because we didn't want to think about what it could *mean*. What we would have to give up.

"I understand if this is unsettling to learn," Blossom said. "I can relate, of course. And as you know, Charlie and Faye will take over as town stewards in three days, on the equinox. None of us knew what had spurred their decision to retire, but what they've been waiting for, all this time, was Jonas. Because now that Jonas is here, now that there is a viable *offering*, they can retire." Her voice was cold and clear.

"In order for Edgewood's protections to remain intact, the cost is Jonas' life," Blossom said. "But each of us gathered here must admit this act is unthinkable. I am bringing this before you because—well, Faye didn't want to burden you with this. But I felt . . . well, we've known most of you all our lives, and you've known us. And I know you cannot expect this—this *vile* thing of my sister. Edgewood is built on a foundation of safety, for everyone. What we *need* is transparency. You all—*we all*—deserve to know the true cost of our safety."

"What will happen if you don't do it?"

I squinted against the firelight and saw that Mr. Tamblin had spoken.

Blossom shook her head. "I don't know. And that's the

truth. But, even if there are consequences, is that the kind of place we want to be? A place willing to sacrifice the innocent life of a child in return for the protection of the majority?"

There was a momentary lull—not silence, because the roar of the katydids vibrated through the trees.

In that brief but terrible emptiness, I noticed a horrifying thing: the way those people, my friends and neighbors, were looking at each other, shame clear on their faces, ascertaining they weren't the only ones who were selfish.

The voices erupted at once. I could only make out some of the noise, but what I heard was enough to confirm my worst fears:

"Will we still be safe?"

"What if our children die?"

"What is the point of living here then?"

"It's one child."

"I don't lock my doors."

"Isn't it worth it?"

Then, finally, "Maybe the chickens are a warning."

Bobby Perkins.

His statement caused silence. He broke away from the crowd.

He was looking right at me, bushy eyebrows bunched together, and I stepped forward on shaking limbs. Jonas was warm against my chest.

"I'm sorry. What?" I said. Bobby had clearly forgotten his promise to keep the chickens to himself.

"Don't you play dumb," Bobby repeated. He turned to face the crowd. "It's worse, you know. They aren't just disappearing. Last night—"

"Bobby, don't," I said, my voice barely a whisper.

But he continued. "Last night I found one of my chickens mangled. Legs had been ripped off—they were gone."

Gone. The word echoed into the falling dusk. A sea of terrified faces stared back at me as the realization of that word and all its implications sank in. *Gone*.

Bobby turned back to me. "Look, I know this is hard to think about, and I don't want to make this any harder on you. But you—your family—you're the stewards of this place. You're supposed to protect it. That's how it works. How it's always worked."

"Jonas is *my* child. *My child*." Panic. The precipice loomed. A wave of dizzy nausea swept over me and I gripped the podium to keep myself upright. "Doesn't that matter? Doesn't *he* matter?"

For the first time tonight, I faced Charlie. I needed him to be my ally. I needed to know we were united.

When our gaze met, everything felt as though it went completely still, like the world had kept on turning and left me behind. Black swirled in my periphery.

He shook his head, ever so slightly.

He mouthed the words, "I'm sorry."

The noise from the townspeople heightened in frequency, their initial low buzz of worry escalated to full-blown terror. My beloved neighbors were quickly transforming into a hungry mob, ravenous for one thing: their entitlement to safety. I stepped away from my family. I placed one hand to Jonas' belly and one to the top of his fuzzy head. There were too many voices shouting at once, too many insects buzzing. I thought I might pass out.

Run.

It was the one thought in my head, the only thing louder than their panicked cries and indignant shouts.

No. Don't run.

Stay.

Fight.

As soon as I thought the word, my senses sharpened. My head cleared.

My mother took my place at the podium. "I'm going to

need you all to calm down. Calm down for just a moment and listen."

"Do you know what it took to get my family here?" someone cried out. "Do you?"

"I'm afraid I don't," my mother said. "And I'm sorry to say I don't know what will happen if Faye and Charlie don't go through with the offering."

The *offering*.

Betrayal burned like bonfire smoke in the back of my throat. I wanted to spit it out at her.

Fight.

But how? What did *fight* mean to me, right then, in that moment?

"We'll put it to a vote."

Blossom spoke with such clarity and strength that the people couldn't help but respond. Their discordant exclamations subsided to a low murmur.

My wild eyes fixed on Blossom. She returned my stare without apology, just the true and earnest faith of hopeful innocence.

I gritted my teeth, swallowed my throbbing heart. Grounded my feet, resisted the urge to run.

Low rumbles from the crowd, as the people absorbed this new information.

"Is that fair?"

From the crowd: "Yes!"

Unanimous.

Blossom cleared her throat. "Alright. By a show of hands, all those against making the required offering?"

I was afraid to look at the crowd, but I did it anyway.

My heart sank.

No more than twenty hands were raised.

My heart softened at the sight of Charlie's mother and my sister's raised. I could have kissed them. I glanced at Charlie but it wasn't clear that he'd noticed and even if he had, his jaw was set. He wouldn't even look at me.

Time seemed to move in slow motion.

"And all those for making the offering?"

The rest of the hands went up. Hundreds of them. A town full.

All those people, all of them with their hands raised. All of them knowingly demanding one thing: my son's life in exchange for their own.

The color had drained from Blossom's cheeks, her lips pulled taut across her face. Her brows were furrowed. This was not the town she knew, or the one she believed in. She shook her head, looked at me, blinked. *I'm so sorry*, she mouthed.

It was far too late for sorry, but I loved her for how certain she had been.

I scanned the hungry crowd.

Fight.

But how? There were so many of them, and only one of me. Only one Jonas.

The sea of raised hands, the swarm of arms and fingers, so entangled in the air they were like a writhing creature, a grotesque beast.

I'd known these people my whole life, and never suspected they were monstrous.

Fight.

An epiphany.

These people knew me, too. They knew that I was kind and mild mannered. They knew I had a tendency to acquiesce, to sacrifice my own comfort for that of another's. I would offer my sweater even when it's cold. I would back down in the face of confrontation. I was the girl who would stay in Edgewood forever despite my secret desire to explore the world beyond. I was the woman who would be a good wife despite my husband's shortcomings.

They *knew* me, or they believed they did.

My shoulders sagged. My head dropped. I pressed my nose to the back of Jonas' head.

I began to cry.

The tears were not difficult to access. All I had to do was stop holding them back. My body quaked with sobs. I dropped to my knees, Jonas hugged close to me in the baby carrier. He squirmed. My body shook violently, wild with agony and rage.

The sweet cinnamon smell of my mother engulfed me as she drew me into her soft warmth. I allowed her to hold me, knowing it would strengthen my cause, tell the story I wanted it to.

Her lips were damp against my ear. "I'm so sorry, my baby. My sweet Faye, my sweet forest fairy. We'll get through this together. We are here with you."

My father's voice boomed from the podium speakers. He had finished lighting the bonfire. His face rippled with an orange glow. "I realize—ah—that this is an unusual start to what is usually a celebratory time." He cleared his throat. "But let's all try to make the most of it."

The mood was altered. The crowd was quiet. The mirth and merriment were dampened with the night's unexpected turn, like dirty dishwater seeping into soil. I clung to my mother's sleeves and looked up at the crowd that had betrayed me, watching the people through a glimmering layer of tears.

They milled around slowly. The sweet and salty smells still hung rich in the air, mingled with the char of bonfire smoke.

But then Bobby Perkins stepped to the fire, his arms full, and he tossed his goods into it. He turned back to the rest of them and spoke the words that invoked our sacred fall ritual: "From abundance, comes abundance."

One person here, another there. Gathering their goods toward the fire's edge. Their voices were quiet and soft, maybe ashamed. *From abundance, to abundance.*

But the familiar words had an effect. The comfort of the ritual had an energizing effect. Their declarations got louder, bolder and more certain: "From abundance, to abundance!"

Someone whooped. The mood of the townspeople shifted rapidly. A couple of young girls giggled. Someone asked for a cup of spiced cider, a man announced he had plenty of kettle corn left. Slowly, unimaginably, the night reignited with energy, with celebration, with mirth and merriment and ceremony.

They'd all moved on from my pain, so quickly, so easily. It wasn't their burden to bear. It was mine.

From abundance, to abundance.

Mine, to theirs.

My insides crumbled. I buried my face into my mother's chest, the last place I wanted to be and yet the first place I'd ever found comfort. I sobbed snot and saliva into her flowered dress, Jonas sandwiched in the carrier between us. He squirmed. The sounds of my cries were muffled by the soft cotton of her dress, drowned out by the buzzing katydids and the voices and laughter that echoed sounds of joyous mockery into the drawing night.

CHAPTER TWENTY-ONE
PRESENT

I T'S DIFFICULT TO fathom how long we've been
walking in this tunnel, feeling our way through the
dark. Jonas has slept for a lot of it, the rhythms of my
movements lulling him. I like having him close against my
chest like this, my beating heart communicating to him
that he is safe. I hope he doesn't feel the anxiety that must
be radiating off my entire being.

I am comforted to know that this moment, at least, I
am able to protect him. Curled up in the baby carrier,
pressed against my breasts: he is where he is meant to be.
I'll fight like hell to keep it that way.

I have taken one break from walking to eat some
granola bars, and to allow Jonas to one good, restful
nursing session without the jostle of my constant
movement. I remained on high alert, my ears attuned to
their new, hypersensitive frequency. The break was short,
and I quickly strapped Jonas back into the carrier and
resumed our journey.

I have become accustomed to this incessant walking.

I have become accustomed to the unending blackness
of this unfathomable dark.

There is something meditative about it. The constant,
rhythmic movement of my legs. The inability to see. The
soft sounds of our intermingled breathing. The grope of my

hands along the hard-packed wall of earth that leads me through this strange tunnel. The soft, padded scuffing of my hiking boots on the ground.

I feel connected to this forest, even as I fear what kinds of horrors it may harbor. I am a forest creature. I do belong here. I feel this, deep in my bones. I belong here. I always have. I know this.

I think the forest knows this, too.

The forest is powerful, but I have power of my own. My power comes from my strength, from the animal instinct that drives me to fiercely protect my son.

There is a part of me that belongs here, down in this ancient dark, in the depths of this primordial soil.

I have adjusted to walking without seeing.

I have learned to rely on more than just sight.

The initial instinct is to resist it.

To crave light.

To wonder at what kind of company darkness keeps, about what might live down here among the roots and worms and rot.

The impulse to find light (any light!) was so strong at first, and I had resisted the pull of this darkness.

But I have become resigned to it, as I have become accustomed to walking, to breathing.

The dark is a resting place. An inner place. My senses are heightened. I can hear everything—even the forest as it grows and dies. I can taste the fire of the earth's core at the base of my tongue, the fresh wormy tang of river water and the nourishing ripeness of soil. I can smell the trees growing, the animals living and birthing and hunting and dying. I can feel the soft caress of the soil and roots beneath my fingers, hear the sweet heartbeat of my baby boy.

Down here, there is truth. There is vulnerability, and in that, liberation. There is no light to bend angles into sharp and convincing illusions. No way for something to appear as other than it is. There is nothing to separate me from myself. From who I am at my core.

The dark envelopes me—envelopes us—like a shroud. Welcomes us.

I feel happy, here in the dark. Safer, maybe more so than I've ever felt. This black cocoon is so reassuring I feel that we could stay down here in this deep dark tunnel forever.

Forever.

Deep in the earth, we are buried like a seed. We can grow, safe and protected, where no harm can reach us. We are where we have been headed all along—the abyss—and it is not a scary place like I'd always imagined. It is a safe place, a dark place. We are removed from those that seek to bring us harm, we are buried beneath the earth, down among the roots and worms. We can burrow through the earth with them, can carve our own path to safety.

Jonas fusses and squirms, tired, finally, of the constriction of the baby carrier.

"Shhhhh," I tell him, and loosen the straps on the carrier just enough to help him find my breast.

Relief washes through me. Safe, we are safe. Truly. Finally. Maybe for the first time, ever. Nothing can touch us down here. Nothing can reach us. No one can take my baby from me, if I can just keep him down in the dark.

Forever.

The thought pulls at me, rich with temptation. How easy it would be to succumb to it, to hide my baby away from the world for eternity. The urge to stay down here in this strange underground tunnel is strong, so strong, and yet beneath that bewitching urge, a deeper thought nags.

Sustenance.

I can't really stay down here forever, can I? (*No, but I want to.*) That isn't really protecting him, is it? Could I really do that, bury myself, bury us, just to shield him from the horrors of the world?

LISA QUIGLEY

The darkness wants to swallow me—and it feels less like being devoured and more like being born. Like being welcomed into a place that has been waiting, looming. (*The precipice.*) The darkness is full and *complete* and it is safe and it is everything and it is home. It has been waiting for me. Like a warm, contained womb, Jonas and I are protected here. (*Forever.*)

Not forever.

I swallow, try to feel the edges of my body, the places where Jonas ends and I begin. I need to protect him, yes, but I cannot contain him, I cannot protect him to the point of suffocation. (*Like my parents did to me.*)

But it's hard to feel anything down here, hard to feel anything but burrowed and buried, hard to feel separate from this wonderful darkness.

Still, I try. The reality is this: if we stay down here forever (*oh but I want to*) we will die. Another deep breath. Not forever then. Just until the equinox. Just long enough. Just until we are safe. (*But will we ever be safe?*)

I feel the reassuring press of cool soil against my back through my jacket, my backpack a comfortable support next to me. Jonas nurses contentedly. I lean my head against the wall of earth, and my body feels suddenly weighted with fatigue. I've been running, in a state of flight, of fighting, of anxiety, ever since my parents told me.

For the first time since then, I'm in a safe place. We can stay here until it's over. Here, we are protected. We have enough provisions to last us at least a little while. I am consumed by a sense of certainty: they will not find this tunnel. They cannot find it. It isn't accessible to them. Only to those who need it. The thought is strange, but it hits me with a force that is so abrupt I know it to be true.

And the realization allows my tense muscles to soften, and as Jonas' strong suction turns to rhythmic flutters, I know that he, too, is falling asleep.

***

112

THE FOREST

Something clicks in the dark.

So many different things ticking in unison, so that their unholy chorus creates a dull buzz. The cacophony approaches.

In a panic, I push myself to stand. Wildly I reach blindly for my backpack until my fingers graze the canvas material. I heft it up and onto my back and still, the clicking is closer.

It's an inhuman sound. An insect sound, I realize now. A torrent of them, all shrieking in unison. Rushing toward me, a flood.

With my fingers grazing the wall for balance, I begin to run.

But it's too late, because the insects—*beetles*—are upon us—*hungry beetles*—and even as I run, they climb up my legs, long wiry legs poking and prodding, feeling and sensing their way through the opening of my shirt sleeves. They burrow into my hair, they are crawling on the baby carrier, on Jonas.

I brush away the insects with large, sweeping motions. Their bodies are hard shells and their mouths pinch my fingers. Their bodies crunch beneath my feet and I am surrounded by these horrible creatures.

Jonas cries out, his wail strangled against my chest, and I continue to flee.

CHAPTER TWENTY-TWO
BEFORE THE FOREST

GIVE THE APPEARANCE of normal.

That was my goal.

But I wasn't sure what "normal" was supposed to look like for a woman whose own family and town—whose own *husband*—had turned against her. A woman who'd agreed to abandon her son to the forest in three days.

Though I'd been completely sober and touched none of Mr. Channing's famous spiced hard cider, my memory of the previous night was distorted like a dream. I'd spent most of the night attempting to keep it together, preventing myself from biting at the fingers that reached out to touch Jonas' milk-soft cheek. To keep the word *traitor* out of my eyes when those same people who had effectively voted to murder my son passed sipping their spiked cider, giving me condolences, sweeping their greedy fingers through the gold-brown curls at the nape of Jonas' neck all while refusing to look directly at me.

Give the appearance of normal.

It was morning, and I was on my side. Jonas suckled at my breast. Charlie was on the couch; I couldn't even look at him last night, let alone feel the betrayal of his body sleeping soundly beside me.

I was deep in thought. Planning. Preparing.

Jonas and I would one chance at escape.

114

THE FOREST

Only one.

We had to make it count. I could not make any mistakes. I had to execute it perfectly. If I got everything today, we could take the car and leave that very night, while the town slept. There was only one road out of town. I had to get it right.

Give the appearance of normal.

The day after the fall festival, I always made chili. So that's where I started.

After Jonas finished nursing and I changed his diaper, dressed and fed him breakfast, I placed him on the floor of our bedroom while I got dressed.

Charlie entered the room just as I was pulling on my jeans over striped underwear. I turned my back to him and he looked to the floor, my state of partial undress uncomfortably intimate in the current state of our marriage.

I felt a stab of pain in my lower belly, as well as a rush of rage at the way my body betrayed me. My heart and my mind were angry with him beyond repair, but my body hadn't caught up yet. My body longed for him, wished to go to him, to feel the wiry black hairs of his chest press against my bare skin. Wished to connect, make everything right again.

But there was no making this right. Not between Charlie and me.

I pulled a grey t-shirt on, covered up my nakedness as though doing so could hide the rest of me.

"Where are you going?" he said.

"Grocery store."

Charlie bent toward Jonas, who was crawling happily on the carpeted floor.

"Don't *touch* him."

"Faye, *please*."

My hands curled into fists and I wanted to scream at him, to beat him with the full force of my rage, until his

115

face looked the way my insides felt. How could he be so heartless?

"Please, what?" I said. I needed to get a handle on myself. *Give the appearance of normal.* But what did normal look like, now?

"I feel terrible," Charlie said. He scooped Jonas up off the floor, crushed the scruff of his beard to Jonas' cheek. Despite my better judgment I made no move to stop him. I stood there, arms limp, my insides screaming against the interior of my skin.

Rage beat against the backs of my eyeballs, felt like it might pummel straight through, and then I was crying.

"I don't know if I can do it," I whimpered.

"It'll be so hard," Charlie said, still holding Jonas close. "But I have hope."

I nodded and wiped my tears. "It hurts." I meant his betrayal, but Charlie heard what he wanted to hear, what *I* wanted him to hear.

"I know," Charlie said. "But we are one family. Jonas is one boy. They are—the town is—well, it's all of them. One life for—all of theirs. It's like Jonas is a—"

"A savior?" It was a struggle to keep the malice from poisoning my tone.

"Yes," Charlie whispered. Then he kissed Jonas' cheek. "Exactly. It's a privilege, really. When you look at it the right way."

"A privilege."

"An honor."

It was true that Edgewood was not a religious town. But I realized in that moment, when I thought of how we valued our ill-gotten, unearned safety, our protection, that we were not without our idols.

"I have to go." I pulled Jonas from Charlie's arms.

"Want to leave him here?"

I stood, slowly, incredulously, and pressed Jonas close to my chest. "He's coming with me."

"Faye."

"What?" My breath hitched in my throat. "If this is the—if these are the last moments—"

But I couldn't finish the thought, I couldn't say the words out loud. They were too rotten in the back of my throat.

"I want to spend time with him, too." Charlie's voice was low, barely a whisper.

Maybe you should have thought of that, I wanted to spit at him. Instead, I said, simply, "I'm his mother."

The words had a solidity—a finality—about them that even Charlie couldn't argue with.

At the front door, with Jonas on my hip, I checked my purse for my wallet and car keys. Charlie hovered near us, his presence a cold dark moon tethered to an aching planet. I looked up at him. There was a deep line etched between his fuzzy black eyebrows. "What is it?"

"You aren't—you wouldn't—?"

"What, Charlie?" I said, exasperated. "Wouldn't what?"

"Wouldn't—leave? Or—try to run?"

I rolled my eyes. "I'm going to the grocery store. It's the middle of the day. I have none of Jonas' things. None of my things."

"But if you're feeling desperate—"

"We need stuff for chili. We'll be back within an hour."

I strapped Jonas into his car seat and the protective measure was ludicrous. The warm autumn sunlight was bright, and I blinked it back. Reality seemed warped: distorted and surreal. The perfect normalcy another betrayal.

I climbed into the front seat of the car and turned it on. Charlie still lingered in the entryway, watched us leave.

I was halfway to the grocery store when the red and blue lights flashed in my rearview mirror. My pulse jumped and I was flooded with another jolt of adrenaline, another message from my body to *run*. No, I reminded myself. Stay. *Fight*.

LISA QUIGLEY

I pulled the car over to the curb.

Sheriff Wilson approached my window. I rolled it down.

"Sheriff Wilson," I said, by way of greeting.

"Faye," he said, and nodded. "Where you headed?"

"I'm sorry," I said, hoping I appeared more perplexed than frightened. "Did I do something wrong? Was I speeding? Did I miss a stop sign or something?"

Sheriff Wilson's mouth curled into a twist. When he spoke, his words were slow and deliberate. "I recognized your car. Of course. We all know what your car looks like."

I held his gaze for a beat. Then, I said, lightly, "Of course."

"I know you had a rough night. I just wanted to make sure you were okay."

I offered my best attempt at a grateful smile. "I've been better."

"Yes, I imagine so. Well, Faye, I just wanted to check up on you and make sure you weren't up to anything . . . *unpleasant*."

"Unpleasant," I said, slowly, the word taking on many shades of meaning. I shook my head, smile weakening. "Just headed to the grocery store. Annual chili."

"You got Jonas with you."

My skin prickled. "I do."

He pulled a handkerchief from his pocket, wiped his brow. "If you and Charlie need anything, you just let us know. I've got Deputy Clark posted up on the Route to keep an eye out for anything—unsavory. You understand."

I did understand. Loud and clear.

"Love that chili of yours."

"Tell you what. You stop by tomorrow evening. I'll set some aside for you to take home to Mrs. Wilson."

"I'm sure she'll appreciate it. You have a good day now."

"You, too."

118

The Forest

Just after he turned back to his cruiser, he glanced over his shoulder. "And, Faye?"

"Yeah?"

"You're gonna do a great job as steward."

"Change is good," I said cheerfully.

"Yeah. Not too much, though."

I shook my head. "Of course not."

"We have faith in you."

"Thank you."

"All right, take care, now."

He climbed into his car, turned the flashing lights off.

I yearned to rest my forehead on the steering wheel but I didn't dare. The whole town was watching me. The sheriff's department was watching me. Everyone knew what our car looked like.

I only had one shot and I had to make it count. If I took the car, they'd be waiting, watching. Ready to follow. Prepared to stop.

I couldn't risk it.

I sucked in a breath of air, trying to soothe the stitch of panic that beat against my ribcage. Because I only had one choice now.

I would have to take Jonas into the forest. On foot.

CHAPTER TWENTY-THREE
PRESENT

THERE IS THE faintest suggestion of light, just ahead. It is so slight, I almost miss it. Or, it's not that I miss it, exactly; it's more like I just mistake it for the strange way the darkness has shifted and moved as my eyes became accustomed to it—maybe even just the hopeful imagining of my panicked brain.

But this is not a trick of my mind, a scrambling to form the darkness into shapes and images that make sense.

I run toward it, the beetles still clicking and crawling and licking. I have given up on moving carefully. My only objective is to get out of this tunnel, release myself and Jonas from the terrible torment of these awful bugs.

The dim light gets closer, closer, until I am almost running through it, and then—my foot hits something solid.

Click-click-click.

The beetles are upon me, crawling across my face and lips and hands.

I flick their giant bodies off and grip the wall to steady my balance. Out, get me *out*.

Even with this adjusted light, it is still too dark to see with any clarity.

With one hand on Jonas' back, I kneel on the ground.

The Forest

I use my hands to feel around for the obstruction, moving hordes of beetles out of the way in the process. When my hands find it, it feels like the lip of a crude stair carved out of hard earth. I reach up, higher, and I am right.

Stairs.

We have reached the end of this underground tunnel.

I look upward, strain my gaze in the direction of the light. Yes. There must be an opening—though likely covered and obscured—because the quality of the darkness is even more muted higher up.

The light at the end of the tunnel.

I don't even give a shit about the obvious cliché and I hurl myself up the stairs, disregarding safety, forgetting about going slow. The beetles crawl and click and lick and bite. Out. *Get us out*.

We climb the stairs and I shove beetles from Jonas' head, from my face, away from my mouth.

It's a tight squeeze at the top, and I have to crouch. With everything I am carrying, we fit—but just barely.

After such complete darkness, this little bit of daylight is enough to illuminate this entire section of the stairway. I grip the edges of the cool slab of rock that hides the tunnel exit and push. It's heavy, but it eventually budges, and I am able to slide the rock open and emerge from the tunnel.

The daylight is sharp and shocking. At first, it physically hurts—the pain a cold white throb in the backs of my eyes. Jonas whines and squirms in the carrier.

"Shhhh," I murmur, and press my lips to the top of his head, my eyes closed. "I know it's bright, baby." The beetles click hungrily.

Jonas settles, and I run my hands over our bodies, shove the beetles off of me, off of *us*, and the light is an abrasion against my eyes, and at first I think they are playing tricks on me. I look at my arms, expecting to see those offensive hard-shelled bodies, but there is nothing.

I stop short. I look behind me into the tunnel, the

daylight illuminating just inside the opening, where thousands of ravenous beetles should be.

Nothing is there.

I run my fingers through my hair, wanting to shake those hard little bodies free—but there is nothing.

No beetles, no bugs, no insects at all. I check Jonas' head, face, hair, run my fingers through the insides of the baby carrier.

But there is nothing. The beetles are gone.

We need to continue on toward the main road. We need to find the next town. We need to find people who will help us.

Still.

It had been a blessed reprieve from the running and the hiding, the constant lookout, the terror of being discovered. I wish I could go back, but I know I can't.

The wet, green smell of decaying leaves and damp moss lurks. It never completely abated. It had been down here with us, following us at a distance, giving us space. I've come to accept this as inarguable fact, and not some wild invention of my imagination. How close it had come to us, how near its breath on my skin before backing away.

Was this—creature?—an enemy?

Did the forest want to help us—or harm us?

Were the beetles a warning? A reminder of what happens when you stay too long in the dark?

The light slants through the trees on an angle. We still have some time before the sun sets, but it is definitely late afternoon.

I chew the inside of my cheek.

Near a cluster of bushes, I feel confident we can rest for a while and remain hidden. Echoes of the beetles' tiny feet reverberate across my body, but when I reach to flick them off, there's nothing. A trick of the imagination.

I lay a blanket on the ground, my ears on high alert listening for the search party. I can't hear anything except for regular forest noises. The distant roar of the river—we must be farther upstream now, where the water gets deep and wild—the hush of the breeze through the treetops. The thumps and scattering of squirrels and chipmunks, the wild calls of the birds. The forest is alive with sound, but none of them are human.

I have no way of knowing where this tunnel has taken us, or how close or far we may be to the main road. But I do know that it served its most urgent and pressing purpose: it allowed us to evade our followers. It doesn't really matter how much lost time we have to make up, because the tunnel saved us. Without it, we would have been captured. This would all be over.

I breathe a small prayer of thanks—to what? To whom? The forest? The trees? The creature? It doesn't really matter; my gratitude is the same regardless. I unhook the baby carrier straps and place Jonas on the ground. He grins delightedly.

"Feels good to get out of there—huh, buddy?" I keep my voice low, but the late afternoon sun feels good and warm and it enlivens me. It feels right to be back among the land of the living. I want to bask in it, to marvel at the way Jonas' smile cuts right into my heart, bursts it wide open.

The tunnel was a stroke of good luck. An omen. We are safe. We are protected. I have never believed in these kinds of things—not on a conscious level, at least—but out here in the forest, it is easy to believe in magic. I touch the wooden beads of my necklace, watch joyfully as Jonas scuttles and scooches on his belly, alternating between attempts at crawling and dragging himself on his tummy.

This is good.

This is right.

We are out here in this wild world, but we are safe. We are meant to escape. We are meant to be free. Why else would I have found that tunnel at just the right time?

Everything is working as it should. I leapt, and the net appeared. I did what I knew in my heart was right. It wasn't easy—it was downright terrifying—but we are here in this beautiful forest, in this perfect, golden autumn light, and it's just Jonas and me, and the aroma of earth and the green, mossy stink of wet autumn leaves, and—

The stink.

I hadn't realized how strong it had gotten once again, and my skin prickles with chill.

I turn around, sharply, expecting to see something—someone?—behind me.

But there is no one.

Just the cloying stench on the breeze, pine needles on the forest floor, wet and rotting.

I breathe slowly.

I am a fool.

I reach reflexively for Jonas, but he is right here in front of me, on his belly, playing with a stray pine cone.

I touch my hand to the small of his back.

We are not yet safe.

We are not yet out of the woods.

CHAPTER TWENTY-FOUR
BEFORE THE FOREST

THE PUNGENT AROMAS of chili powder and cumin spice filled my kitchen. There was a row of Tupperware containers on the counter next to the stove. I usually found the chili smell to be warm and comforting, a hearty reminder of fall. That day, it was a stink, a stench, thick and cloying. It was too much sensation. Too *much*.

Jonas had pulled all the tea boxes off the little shelf in the corner of the kitchen. My heart squeezed at the sight of him yanking each individual tea packet from them. It was in those unassuming moments that my pain was most acute. Tea packets were nothing to most of us, were commonplace, ordinary, a means to an end, something to be carelessly discarded. To Jonas, they were colorful, crinkly packages of paper delight just for him. That's what I loved most about being a mother: watching my son thrive in his process of discovery and wonder.

It's also what hurt the most.

I stirred my simmering pot of chili and the thick liquid resisted my wooden spoon. I never noticed before how much chili looked like garbage. What was the difference between the mess that accumulated at the bottom of the sink when we cleared our dinner plates, and the slop in the pan before me?

Chili was usually one of my favorite things about fall—but my appetite had soured. Objectively, I could tell that it smelled good—it smelled *right,* it's *my* chili—but savory tastes were a meaningless luxury, an arbitrary delight. *Flavor* felt like a gross abomination. Ordinary indulgences seemed needlessly extravagant. The hearty pot may just as well have been seasoned with poison as spices.

Ten sleeping pills were in my pocket, their presence a heavy weight on my conscience. I was afraid Charlie would smell my shame, thick and hearty as the aroma of the chili. I'd never done anything like this before. I wasn't sure of the right amount. I didn't want to kill him. I just wanted him to sleep long enough to give Jonas and me a fighting chance.

I took a deep, exaggerated breath, wiped at the thin layer of sweat on my upper lip.

Act normal.

The thought was as absurd as it was vital. It all felt so utterly ridiculous and I was struck with a sudden and unbearable urge to laugh. How nonsensical it all was, me standing there in the kitchen, my son playing on the floor, chili bubbling on the stove as though everything was alright, as though it were just any ordinary day. My breath caught and just as quickly I was biting back tears.

Get a hold of yourself.

Act normal.

Normal.

Fuck.

Charlie darkened the kitchen doorway. Him and his hovering. I wanted to scream. Instead, I nodded at him curtly and reached for a Tupperware container.

"Saw Sheriff Wilson on my way into town," I said, scooping a ladle of chili into the plastic cylinder.

"Oh?" Charlie sounded puzzled. "Was he at the grocery store?"

"I told him I'd set some chili aside for him and Mrs. Wilson. She's a big fan."

The Forest

"I didn't take Sheriff Wilson for a big grocery shopper."

"Says he'll stop by tomorrow to pick it up," I said, and held up a finger. "I will label *one* for you, for work. Make sure you take the right one. Leave the others alone."

"I hope Mrs. Wilson is feeling alright."

"Are you even listening?"

"You'll label one for my lunch. Got it."

His presence was stifling. The way he blocked the exit felt menacing. I thought of Sheriff Wilson pulling me over. I thought of his thinly veiled threat. Everyone wanted to trap me there. Even Charlie. What was worse was they'd been trapping me my whole life. I swallowed and set my jaw, lifted my chin. It was a subtle movement, a steeling of my resolve within myself. I didn't want Charlie to read my defiance and decipher it. But I refused to let anyone stand in my way. Not my parents, not my siblings, not our neighbors, not Sheriff Wilson. Not my husband.

I could almost taste the bitterness of the sleeping pills in my pocket. My mouth watered.

He wouldn't smell my determination. The aroma of the chili was too cloying, too deceptive. It was right. It was exactly as it should be. I'd made sure of it. I was my mother's daughter, after all.

I met Charlie's eyes. I offered a tentative smile. I was thinking about my plan, every last detail, how it would be hard, but we would make it. Because I was Jonas' mother and I had to protect him. My love, my utter determination was stronger than all of them put together. That had to count for something. It would work. It had to.

My smile was genuine.

CHAPTER TWENTY-FIVE
PRESENT

WHEN I FINISH nursing Jonas and tuck my empty food wrappers into the backpack, I let Jonas wiggle around on the blanket a little bit longer. I know that he enjoys being in the baby carrier, that he watches with wide eyes as the world goes by. Even so, I can't help but feel guilty, like I'm keeping him cooped up all day while I walk. *It's for his own good.* I know that, but I also know that he's a baby, and there's no way I can communicate that to him in a way he will understand. I only hope that somehow, with his heart pressed up against mine, the beating of my own will communicate my earnest love for him in a way that words can't, yet.

The angle of the light through the trees sharpens, the quality of the light more golden. This makes me nervous. The sun isn't setting yet, and it won't for a few more hours, but it gets dark faster in the forest. I wasn't anticipating another night in the forest, and while the underground tunnel saved our lives, I have no idea where it led us, or how far out of the way we might be.

While Jonas scuttles around on his belly in our makeshift shelter, I dig into my pocket for the compass.

The needle skips erratically across the face. It won't settle.

I tap the face, shake it lightly.

Still, the needle dances.

I turn in a half circle and check again, and again, and again.

Without a working compass, we really are lost out here.

My throat tightens as panic wraps icy fingers around it.

Jonas has found another pinecone, and he is about to stick it into his mouth. I crouch and pull it away from his mouth. "Don't eat that," I whisper. I toss it into the bushes and he returns to his investigation of the blanket in our little thicket.

I feel, suddenly, so tired. The ups and downs are getting the better of me. I won't let this terrible dark anxiety have me. Not now. Not while I have Jonas to protect.

I retrieve my worn map from the backpack. Without a compass, the map is useless—but still. There might be something that can help me figure out where I am.

Jonas coos over a pine needle. The sound makes me smile.

I trace my fingers over the worn lines of the map I've looked at so many times, but a rock builds and solidifies in the pit of my stomach.

None of this tells me anything.

I know that I am in the forest, that's all. I look up. Blue sky through the canopy of faded green and brilliant yellow. Sunlight, sharp and golden, on a slant through the branches. Dust motes catch in the jagged gashes of light. My breath hitches in my throat.

I feel so lost.

We have come so far, to only be stranded.

Without the compass, I feel unmoored, untethered. Disconnected from any chance of hope. We are so small, and the forest is so large, and so unending. The forest is wild and unforgiving.

I try to remember how I felt, down in the dark, when I

knew that I belonged here, when I knew that I was also something ancient and wild.

But up here, in the harsh reality of daylight, I am small. I am not connected to eternity. I am not infinite.

I am human.

I'm just a mother, desperate to save her child.

The forest doesn't care about me. I am not special.

Jonas makes an inquisitive sound. My breasts tingle, filling with milk on instinct.

Something inside me melts, softens, surrenders.

I don't know who I am, or if I am truly a part of something bigger than myself, but none of that matters.

Because I am special, to someone.

To Jonas.

He needs me.

I am not just me, and he is not just Jonas. We are mother and son. We are a dyad, two creatures existing in tandem. We need each other to survive.

We need each other.

I stand, turn my face to the sky. I close my eyes. Feel the gentle bite of the autumn breeze against my face.

I breathe in, slowly, let the air fill the empty spaces between the panic.

Jonas scoots over to me, and his fingers pull at the laces on my hiking boots.

I feel the tug of his hands, and I listen.

Rustling of the wind through the trees. Creaking of ancient trunks in a gentle sway. Chirping of birds. Roaring river. Scratching of squirrel claws across the bark on branches.

Jonas tugs and coos.

The river.

I open my eyes.

I bend down again to look at the map.

I trace my finger along the river, observe the way it curves through the forest.

THE FOREST

There is a point where the river meets the road.

It's a farther distance than I had hoped to walk, and it's not as direct as my original plan of cutting through the forest to meet the main road on the other side. It will be a longer journey—at least another day.

It's not ideal. But it's an option—our *only* sure way out of this forest, without the compass. The fact that it has gone haywire shouldn't bother me so much—compasses can break, can't they?—but it's unsettling. Why now? Why today? What made it stop working? Or *who*?

I strap Jonas back into the baby carrier and give him his pacifier to soothe his quiet protests. He was really enjoying his romp on the ground and isn't happy that I want him to end it so quickly. The pacifier works, though, and he curls himself against me, his eyes going soft and sleepy as they always do when he is close to me.

The roar of the river—fast and violent—is present, an undercurrent of sound that bathes the forest with white noise.

Sound is tricky, though, especially here. The way the sound echoes and ricochets off the trees, it's difficult for me to pinpoint the exact direction. In some moments, it sounds like it is definitely to my right. In others, definitely to my left. I tense. I scan the canopy of trees with my eyes.

And then I notice it. A clearing? Could it be the road? Is it possible that the tunnel took us farther than I had originally thought, that I am already approaching the end of our journey?

My footsteps are careless. Twigs snap beneath my boots, leaves crush and crinkle. The rush of the river gets louder, roars like blood in my ears.

I am closer to the clearing now. I am daring to hope, even though I know it is foolish. Daring that when I reach the last clump of trees, I will emerge to see the road just beyond the opening. I dream of walking along that stretch of highway, of following it into the next town. I think of the

131

money in my wallet, and of finding a diner like I have read about in books, watched in my favorite tv shows. I will order a stack of pancakes and drown them in syrup. I'll let Jonas taste them, too—a special occasion.

Jonas can sense my desperation, my eagerness, my hunger. He whines softly, but the approaching roar of the river drowns out his cries.

I clear the last line of trees, step into the clearing—and gasp.

We stand on a steep cliff overlooking the river. A rush of vertigo hits me at the sight of the sharp dropoff that looms at the edge. My body tenses instinctively and, reflexively, I place my hand to Jonas' back.

CHAPTER TWENTY-SIX
BEFORE THE FOREST

EVERY MUSCLE IN my body protested, but I allowed Charlie to take Jonas into the living room. I needed Charlie out of the kitchen. I couldn't see him, but was reassured by Jonas' delighted coos. Charlie may have been the worst kind of monster—the kind hidden beneath the ordinary skin of the human man I thought I loved—but he wouldn't *actively* hurt Jonas.

My mind sent me intrusive images: Charlie implanting a tracking device beneath Jonas' skin. Charlie slipping out the front door, Jonas in tow, keeping him from me until it's too late. I resisted the urge to run into the living room.

Charlie was a mystery to me, now. I didn't truly know *what* he was capable of. Jonas' sweet soft voice was a lifeline.

I scooped ladles full of chili into two white porcelain bowls.

I prepared Charlie's plate every night, so nothing about this was out of the ordinary. Disgust filled me. I'd been a *good* little housewife. How foolish I had been. One consolation: my naivety would pay off tonight. It had to.

With shaking fingers, I pulled the pills from my pocket. *Give the appearance of normal. Get it together.* I placed three tablets onto the cutting board and used the heel of a knife to mash them into fine white powder.

133

Deftly, I swept the powder into Charlie's bowl. Picked up a spoon and stirred. Steam curled from the bowl, lifting the chili stink to my nostrils.

I gathered the cutting board and the spoon into the sink. The faucet squealed when I turned it on. I rinsed the powder off the cutting board, washed away the evidence. I rinsed the spoon and put everything into the dishwasher, turned it on despite it being only halfway full.

"Should you wait to run it till after we've added dinner dishes?"

Charlie's voice made me jump and I looked up to see him in the kitchen doorway again. He was holding Jonas, dark stubble pressed to Jonas' round cheek. I wanted to peel my baby from him, but I resisted the impulse.

I carried the steaming bowls of chili to the kitchen table. "Raw turkey meat on the cutting board," I said. "I want to sterilize it. We can run it again."

"Sure," Charlie said.

He watched me place the chili fixings on the table: a dish of shredded cheddar cheese, sour cream, bright green slices of avocado, a basketful of warm corn bread.

"Get Jonas in his high chair?" I said without looking up.

Charlie put Jonas in his chair, pulled him over to the table, and sat in the chair next to him. The poisoned bowl of chili waited.

He clipped Jonas' seat strap into place and I placed two empty wine glasses on the table. I couldn't drink anything—I needed a clear, focused head—but we always had red wine with dinner. If we didn't have any, Charlie would know something was off. Although, how could things be anything *but* "off"? How were we doing such a mundane thing as eating dinner, when our son's life was at stake? A hot rush of rage turned my belly sour.

Deep breaths.

Give the appearance of normal.

134

I poured the wine and sat down, scooted my chair closer to the table.

Charlie scooped sour cream into his bowl of chili, sprinkling cheese and avocado across the top. I crumbled a piece of cornbread onto Jonas' high chair tray. He picked up a piece, jerkily—he still hadn't full mastered the pincer grasp—and smashed it into his mouth. He smacked his lips together happily. I never knew before what delightful sounds an eating baby could make.

Charlie lifted a spoonful of chili to his mouth. I tried not to hold my breath. My heart hammered in my chest and I chastised myself: I should have taken a tiny taste, made sure the pills hadn't altered the flavor. What if he could taste them? What if he knew something was off? He caught my eye, paused with the spoon poised in front of his open mouth. *Stop watching him.*

I busied myself with preparing my own chili. I was focused on my toppings, but I still saw Charlie out of the corner of my eye. He had taken a bite and was chewing.

"Is it good?" I asked. "Is it . . . right?"

Charlie swallowed. Licked his lips. Squinted his eyes. He smiled. "It's great, babe. Maybe your best yet. There's a reason your fall chili is famous." He took another bite.

I offered a smile. "It's the secret ingredient."

Everyone knew my "secret ingredient" was pumpkin. Charlie smirked, and took another bite. I relaxed a little into my chair. This was going to work.

But then Charlie's spoon was headed in the wrong direction, not toward his own mouth, but toward Jonas'. I cried out before I could stop myself.

"No!" I shrieked. Panic made my voice raw and ragged.

Charlie paused, bewildered, the spoon in midair, hovering just in front of Jonas' lips.

I tried to collect myself, reached for Charlie's arm, gently pushed it away. "Don't you think it's too spicy? It could hurt him."

Charlie's eyebrows furrowed as he considered this. "Oh," he said, and he moved the spoon back toward his bowl. A drop of red liquid splashed onto Jonas' tray. I wiped it away with a napkin. "I hadn't thought of that."

"Clearly."

Charlie balled his hand into a fist, pressed it to his lips before he spoke. "Did you have to freak out like that? You scared the shit out of me."

"We're used to the spice. Sorry. There's just a lot of cayenne in this. I don't think he's ready."

Charlie shrugged. "I was just thinking maybe you'd like him to taste it, before—before—" but Charlie couldn't look at me, and he didn't finish his sentence. He went back to eating.

Before you murder him. I inhaled slowly, tried to still my racing heart.

I watched Charlie clean his bowl out of the corner of my eye, and I didn't feel sorry at all.

It happened quicker than I had imagined. Charlie was reaching for another piece of cornbread, but I noticed that he was moving slower than usual. He plucked the cornbread from the breadbasket, but he moved as though it were disproportionately heavy. His arm sagged beneath the weight of it.

"You okay?" I said.

Charlie's eyebrows bunched up in the center. "I'm, just," he said. His words came out slow, slurred like he was talking through the thick mouthful of the honey he'd just slathered on his cornbread. He dropped it onto his plate, lifted his hands slowly to either side of his head. "Feel . . . weird."

"Maybe you should go lay down." I tried to sound more concerned than I was. Really, I had begun running through a mental checklist of everything I needed to do once he was fully out.

"Bubble turnip," Charlie said, or something that sounded like it.

136

The Forest

I went to him, hooked my shoulder beneath his armpit and tossed his arm around my neck. I helped him stand, but it was difficult, because he was already mostly deadweight. Somehow, I managed to help him half walk, half drag himself into the living room and onto the couch. He collapsed onto it. He looked up at me, eyes muddy and betrayed.

"Good night, Charlie," I said.

I just hoped that three pills were enough to keep him out for as long as I needed, but not too much to kill him.

It was getting dark out, and the living room window was a great dark eye, exposing me. I hoped no one could see me. I closed the front curtains with a frantic swish.

I returned to Jonas and cleaned him up. Then I carried him with me into the bedroom, where I would get everything ready.

Now the real work could begin.

Chapter Twenty-Seven
Present

THE CLIFF IS about fifteen to twenty feet above the river, and juts directly over white, swirling, rushing waters. This section of the river is deep, and fast. I move another inch forward and a clump of dirt loosens, tumbles over the edge.

I survey the white ribbon of the river that stretches, long and curling, into the forest.

I hadn't *really* believed we could have made it to the road already. And yet, a small part of me had hoped I would step into this clearing and the road would be visible through the trees.

I inhale the smell of wet earth and damp moss. The subtle green stink of rotting leaves.

Then I hear it: a shout.

Another.

A *human* shout.

I scan the edges of the river, prodding, searching. My chest tightens with panic and I hear the shouts again, louder this time.

And then I see them.

The search party is just a bit farther upstream along the river, and they have spotted us out in the open on the river's edge.

I back away, slowly.

The Forest

We can run, we can hide in the forest. If I can just make it to the entryway, we can hide out in the tunnel until they are gone, until they lose our scent.

My breath catches, because there is movement in the trees just ahead.

They are fast. They aren't that far away on the riverbank now—so many of them and just two of us.

They move between me and the woods.

We are trapped.

I back up, acutely aware of the cliff, wide and menacing behind me like an open mouth full of sharp teeth.

They spot me again, and they are still on the move.

This is it, then.

I expect Jonas to cry, but he is still, and snuggled into my chest. His perfect peace feels incongruously calm against this terrible moment.

They are getting closer.

They will catch us. It's inevitable now.

There are only two options, neither of them good.

I can allow them to catch us, or I can jump off the cliff and into the river.

The thought of it tangles my insides. It's risky. I could hurt Jonas. But if they catch us, then Jonas is guaranteed to be hurt.

I inch closer to the edge. I look over and feel dizzy. My legs shake and tingle.

We are high, but we are not at a dangerous distance.

My friends and family encroach upon us.

I shrug the backpack off my shoulders.

I place one hand over the back of Jonas' head, and with the other hand, I pinch his nose closed.

Then I jump.

CHAPTER TWENTY-EIGHT
BEFORE THE FOREST

I DIDN'T KNOW how much time I had, so I moved like I was rapidly running out of it. I couldn't afford to take much. Just what I could carry on my back.

I gathered what I would need for Jonas first. Extra onesies, layers of warmer clothes. The baby carrier. Fruit and vegetable baby food pouches. Luckily he was still nursing, and I knew he could subsist primarily on milk.

For myself, I packed a sweatshirt, a couple changes of underwear, socks, an extra t-shirt and pair of pants.

I filled the medium sized, waterproof backpack with two warm blankets, a flashlight, a compass, several books of matches. A tin cup and plate that we had our small camping excursions.

I collected the folded maps from underneath our bed, opened them for the first time in years. I studied the possible routes through the forest, to where the other end of the tree line meets the far side of the main road. I took a deep breath. I could do this. I refolded the maps, tucked them carefully into the backpack so I could study them when I was away.

Packing the bag made me smile—wistfully—to remember the girl I once was. This wasn't the first time I'd tried to run away—but it was the first time it mattered that I get it right.

The Forest

I was nervous about food and water. I didn't know how long I'd be in the forest for, or how long it would take me to reach the main road on the other side. I was hoping it wouldn't be longer than three days, but I had no idea what I was up against. And they'd be after me. I wouldn't have much time before it was too late.

I filled a large water bottle and brought the water purification tablets we had leftover from last year's camping trip. "Camping trip" didn't really describe it, because it wasn't like we really went anywhere. Merely a weekend campout in the peripheral woods with friends and family, always within Edgewood's borders. Charlie always brought the tablets with us "in case of emergency"—which, of course, never happened in Edgewood.

Sometimes it was hard to remember that Charlie hadn't grown up there, and he still had habits from his old life he couldn't shake.

I included a can opener and a few cans of beans, though already I was nervous about the bag being too heavy. With Jonas strapped on my front and the pack to my back, I was already going to be weighed down.

Still food was non-negotiable. I gathered granola and cereal bars from the pantry. These were lighter to carry and would provide calories. If it were only me, I wouldn't be so worried. But I needed to make sure I got enough calories and water to produce milk for Jonas. Then again, if it were only myself, I wouldn't be leaving in the first place.

I tried not to think about this.

I was almost ready. Jonas was fussing and I took a brief break to nurse him. I scooped him from his spot on the floor and sat on the edge of the bed. I lifted my t-shirt, and he suckled at my breast. I was impatient at the delay. Jonas needed to be fed, I knew this, and usually I craved those slow, intimate moments with him. But I didn't know how much time I had left. What if Charlie woke up? What if someone decided to stop by?

Watching his rhythmic swallows calmed me, reminded me why I was doing this. His innocence was a tangible thing, and so was my need to protect him. I *was* doing the right thing.

I tried not to think of the forest.

The forest.

What was it my mother had said?

"The forest demands it."

Wasn't the forest the very thing that demanded my son from me?

And I was just going to walk right into it, let it swallow us up?

I closed my eyes.

If the forest wanted my son, it was going to have me, too.

CHAPTER TWENTY-NINE
PRESENT

I KICK WITH all my might, shoving our bodies toward the surface of the river. I am grateful for the baby carrier that keeps Jonas and me closely tethered, but I don't trust it. I keep one arm around his body and use the other to swim with fierce determination.

The roar of the water calms some, and our bodies break the surface. I gasp for air and Jonas wails—his cry muffled only by the shriek of rushing water—and relief warms me. The current is strong but the water is calmer, and I manage to stay on my back to keep Jonas' face above water. The current is a good thing: the faster it moves, the closer we are to our destination; the farther away from our pursuers.

And yet, despite the blessing in disguise this river has provided, the water is cold, and our position is precarious. These waters are unpredictable, and I don't want to keep Jonas in the river for too long. I look down at him and my heart sinks. His lips are already turning purple around the edges.

There are so many things to focus on at once: staying on my back; keeping Jonas' face above water; kicking to keep us afloat and move us toward the shore. It's too much and I can't look everywhere at once, can't do everything at once.

I am making progress, getting closer to the shore, almost—

The drop is sudden.

As far as waterfalls go, it's not big—but I am unprepared. The back of my head smacks—hard—against a rock before I am able to regain control of my position on my back. Jonas bleats and shivers—he is cold, wet, and agitated.

I am dizzy.

The back of my head throbs with an icy cold pain. It hurts even worse when I turn my head in the direction of the shore.

A wave of nausea hits me when I kick my legs. I am moving toward the shore, I think—I am disoriented and the golden light that filters in at a sharp angle between the trees hurts my eyes. Has it been this bright this whole time? My foot scrapes against the bottom of the river; it catches, and I heave us forward. Standing vibrates my skull. The water's depth recedes to my waist now, then level with my thighs, and, finally, only my knees. I bend over and throw up over Jonas' head.

The trees dance and swirl around me, a kaleidoscope of color and light. I don't know where I am. A hand reaches out and steadies me. I grasp the outstretched arm, allow myself to be guided away from the river's edge, and the person who's helping me—a very nice person, I think—wears a large black cloak. There is a smell like dead leaves and I dissolve into hysterical giggles.

I struggle to stay upright and Jonas cries. My worry is vague and distant.

"He's cold," I say, and cling to the arm at my side.

It really does smell like moss here, like pine needles and leaves decaying on the forest floor, a thick green smell. It's so familiar, so comfortable, and I am so sleepy.

"I need to nurse him," I say, but the arm at my side is firm and steady, it doesn't allow me to slow down. It's leading me somewhere, this arm in the black cloak, and the light hurts my eyes and I think I might throw up again, but

I keep walking. Jonas cries and his shivering body burrows into my chest.

"Shhhhh, baby. Shhhhhh, Mommy's here, Mommy's *here*, and we're going to sleep soon."

My free hand flies to my throat. My necklace is gone, and I laugh some more. I laugh so hard I can barely breathe, can barely walk, but the arm is strong and it holds me up.

"The arm," I say, and I laugh again, but something is wrong. Beneath my strange laughter lies a deep uneasiness. I can't remember who took my arm but I could have sworn I knew them, that I recognized them when they reached for me and that everything is alright, everything is going to be okay. But something's wrong, and I am so tired, and we are in a clearing now, and the arm stops, the arm lets go.

I drop to my knees. My vision is disjointed, strobe-like. My movements are photographic stills of actions, not something I'm actually doing in real time. My body is disconnected from me and the thought terrifies me until I look down, see that I am still me and Jonas is still screaming and my head pounds.

Jonas.

He needs to nurse.

Through all my confusion, this thought comes clearly.

I unhook the baby carrier and coax my crying baby to my chest. Latching soothes him and he settles, but his skin still feels cold and wet, and I can't remember how we got here.

We are in a small clearing, and the light that comes through the trees is so sharp and bright that I squint to keep the headache away. I have the sudden feeling that I'm not alone but when I look around, there is no one in the clearing with us. It is just Jonas and me.

I can't remember how I got here. I thought I remembered someone—a hand—but nothing makes sense right now, nothing is adding up correctly and I feel so dizzy and so tired. I lower my body to the ground and lie on my side, curl Jonas' body into mine and nurse him.

I just need to close my eyes for a minute, a few moments of rest so I can clear my head.

Just before sleep comes, I reach up to touch the Rowan necklace, but it's still gone.

PART TWO

DESIRE

CHAPTER THIRTY

IT HAD BEEN my idea to build the treehouse, but it had been Dad's to make it look like a pirate ship. Dad, Arrow, and I spent nearly every day that summer in the backyard building it, the fresh scent of the pine sap mingled with cut grass and summer clover to create one of the most dizzyingly happy scents of my life.

Once it was built, I could have lived out there. On the warmest nights, I did.

The *treeship* belonged to all of us, but it felt like mine. I would sit in the space the three of us had built together, inhale the fresh-cut wood smell and watch the fireflies illuminate the night, scattered bits of magic fairy light in velvety summer darkness. I took it all in through one of the three circular portholes my father had carefully carved into the treeship's hull. The lightning bugs blinked golden light between the shadows of the trees until my eyes grew tired and my face stretched and expanded with yawning. Then I'd curl up at the bow of my ship, beneath the wheel, a pillow snuggled under my head. The cricket's soft forest songs lulled me to sleep.

One night in particular stands out in my memory.

I was on my back, breathing in that warm sweet honeysuckle air, listening to the rustle of soft summer breath through the trees and the rush of the river in the woods behind our house, when there was a new sound.

An incongruous one.

149

It was the sound of my parents' voices, slipping through an opened window at the back of the house, carrying across the darkness.

I couldn't hear every word, but I could hear their tone, sense their unhappy cadence.

These were not pleasant words. These words were filled with tension.

My parents didn't fight often. I tilted my head to try to hear but could only catch disjointed fragments.

Her: " . . . never going . . . isn't right . . . fill . . . head . . . "

Him: " . . . missing the . . . about imagination . . . dreams . . . "

Her: " . . . aren't safe . . . dissatisfaction . . . want to . . . isn't realistic . . . "

Him: " . . . not everything has to . . . about joy . . . "

The words felt heavy with importance and I had a horrible gnawing suspicion I was at the center of this fight somehow, but I couldn't put all the pieces together, was missing the essential core of the puzzle.

Eventually my parents' voices slowed, then waned, then stopped altogether. The fight ended. The night quieted, resumed its regular soft summer music.

Then I heard a new noise in the dark, a muffled, rhythmic sound. The soft padding of footsteps in the grass, getting closer. Then the creaking of the wooden ladder that poked up through the hole in the floor of the treeship.

I shifted my weight toward the sound, lifted my head so I could eye the dark mouth at the bottom of my boat that opened up to the real world below.

The top of my father's head poked through, the shine of his eyes gleaming in moonlight, his features shrouded in nighttime shadows. There was a funny look on his face, though I couldn't place the expression. I had never seen it before.

His cheeks were red and swollen—he'd been crying. My

father was no stranger to emotion but the thought of those tears, mixed with the weird look—it was a *haunted* look.

"You okay, kid?"

His steady, familiar voice was a soft reassurance in the dark.

I leaned my head back on my soft pillow. Thought before I responded. *Was* I okay? I didn't like to hear them fight, or the way it made me feel. But *how* was that, exactly? Untethered. *Unmoored.*

Instead of answering, I shrugged, even though I wasn't sure if he could see me in the dark.

"I'm sorry if you heard that." My dad paused. "Your mother and I love each other. We love you."

I nodded. Whatever discomfort I may have been feeling, these words rang true.

"We both want what's best for you. For *all* of you."

He didn't stop talking so much as trail off. There were other words that carved negative space into the air between us, things he wasn't saying out loud. But I could feel those words all the same. They were tinged with something like regret, and whatever it was he wanted to say started with the word *Except* . . .

Except he didn't say it.

Except there was no way I could decipher what it was he really wanted to say.

I turned my head, so our shining eyes met in the dark. *Except what, Dad?* I wanted to say, but didn't. Couldn't.

He held my eyes with his gaze, smiled softly. His smile held resignation, and I knew then that he wasn't going to say any more. The moment had passed. We were done for tonight.

"Don't stay out too late, kid. You never know what's lurking in those woods."

I didn't go back into the house that night. I stayed up for a long time, listening to the summer night-song of the forest, and for the first time in my life, the sound was

LISA QUIGLEY

ominous. For the first time in my life, I wondered whether the forest that surrounded us was our protection or our prison. Was there a difference?

What was lurking in those woods?

Bears? Cougars? Other wild animals?

Or was it something else altogether?

What was it that made Edgewood so special?

What kept Edgewood so safe?

I don't know how long I lay awake like that, listening in the dark, turning those disquieting questions around in my mind, never finding any satisfactory answers.

I did know that as I finally drifted off to sleep, I wished that my pirate ship might drift too, and carry me off somewhere new. Somewhere mystery and adventure might await.

Somewhere I might be free.

CHAPTER THIRTY-ONE

WHEN MY FATHER pulled back into town in his beat-up old black truck—with packages of toilet paper piled to the top of the weathered camper shell—the whole town breathed a sigh of relief.

I was fifteen years old, and it was only the second time anyone had ever left our town that I could remember.

He hadn't been gone long—only a week—but it had seemed an eternity. The world outside of Edgewood was unfathomably vast, even more so knowing that it was outside our bubble of protection. There were an infinite number of terrible things that could happen to a person in the world outside, and all week my chest had been tight with worry.

If I was being honest, a small bit of that tension was the product of envy.

More than a small bit.

My mother had seen it in my eyes when I watched the main road. I caught her looking at me, and the fear had been as visible on her face as I knew the longing was on mine. Neither of us had time to wipe our expressions away before the other saw. We stood there for a moment, eyes locked, our cheeks burning red with the shame of being caught.

Later, I tried to play it off like I was worried about Dad. And it was true, I *was*. I just wasn't *only* worried.

And my mother knew it.

What she didn't know was that the night before he left, I had asked him to let me go, too. He'd refused—couldn't put me at risk, he said—and it was the only time I could remember that my father and I had ever fought.

"You don't know what I've gone through to keep you kids safe," he'd snarled, face raw with emotions I didn't understand, ones I was never meant to see. I was too startled to keep fighting, and I stormed off. I'd slept the night in the treeship, a thing I hadn't done since I was a little girl.

I didn't give him a hug before he left or even say goodbye. It ate at me until he returned.

Our regular shipment of toilet paper had been delayed for three weeks due to a manufacturing mishap.

Edgewood was protected from misfortune, but the same wasn't to be said of the rest of the world. We'd experienced minor delays of outside goods before, but nothing this severe. The toilet paper shortage was a serious concern.

As steward, Dad volunteered to make a run into a nearby town. As it turned out, the manufacturing mishap hadn't just affected us, but the entire neighboring area as well. It took him a week to find enough to hold our whole town over until the modified delivery date.

By the time he returned, my usually calm and collected mother was wound like a tight ball of yarn, a tangle of nerves and anxiety. I could almost see her unravel when my dad pulled into the driveway, but she pulled herself back together. I felt a change in the air, too, like the whole town had finally relaxed.

I wondered how many of them felt as I did: burning with curiosity, hot to the touch with questions.

My mother ran to him when he stepped out of the truck and my parents embraced. I didn't leave the doorway. I wasn't angry with my father—in fact, the sight of him filled me with both relief and regret—but rather, I feared that if I got too close, all my questions might come spilling out.

I was afraid that if anyone heard—anyone but my father—they might learn how deep my curiosity ran, might decipher how badly I wanted to explore beyond the borders of Edgewood.

So I stayed in the doorway, my arms folded across my chest, meeting my father's apologetic gaze, my chest swelling with questions.

It wasn't until after my mother had gone to bed—early, exhausted from a long week of worry—that he gave me the maps.

At first, I didn't get what they were.

He placed them on my desk in my bedroom, where I sat doing my homework in the yellow lamp light.

"Sorry you couldn't come."

"Couldn't?" I said, some of the old bitterness resurging in spite of myself.

"Come on, Faye, you know I'd never forgive myself if . . ."

"It's fine. I get it." Even though I didn't. Even though he'd come back just fine. It didn't seem that the outside world was all that dangerous, after all. Safety seemed like such a small price to pay not to be trapped in our suffocating town.

I unfolded the top map, traced my fingers along the unfamiliar lines.

"What are these for?" I said.

"For you."

"Duh. But why?"

"You're curious." My dad looked sheepish, wistful, maybe even regretful. But regretful of what? "These might help."

I was struck with such a fierce stab of longing that for a moment, it was difficult to breathe. It was the coolest gift anyone had ever gotten for me. Treasures from the outside. Proof that there was more to life than this.

I folded the map back up, quickly, afraid to show how

much this meant to me. "Thanks," I said, my voice too sharp with the tears I was holding back.

"You like them?"

"They're cool."

My dad laughed. "High praise from a teenager."

I smiled, afraid that if I laughed, I would cry.

My dad reached out, touched my cheek. "I know it's hard."

I didn't respond, just looked at him.

"All of it," my dad said, reading my mind. "Being here, not understanding why. We're your parents. You know? We just want to do what's best. Keep you safe. Do you get that?"

I nodded, afraid my voice would betray me. A tear slid down my cheek despite my best efforts.

"It's your choice, you know."

My head snapped up, tears threatening to spill over. "What do you mean?"

"Right now, we're your parents, and we're responsible for you, and you're here because it's what we think is best. That's what parents do for their children. Protect them the best way they know how."

"Dad, I—"

He held up his hand. "But one day you'll have a choice. And whatever else you may think—whatever anyone may try to tell you, it's *your* choice. You don't have to stay. You don't have to be town steward. You are free. *Free.* You are. Even if it doesn't feel like it. Even if anyone—*anyone*—tells you different. You hear me?"

I nodded.

"Faye?"

"I hear you."

"Good." He pulled me into a hug, held me like that for a long time. Then he kissed me on the head and left me there in my bedroom with my crisp maps that smelled like fresh paper and ink and mystery and magic.

The Forest

For the first time, I felt the weight of choice on my shoulders. It didn't feel like a burden, something I had to carry.

It felt like something I could lean into.

Something that would carry me.

Chapter Thirty-Two

WHEN I GOT home that night, my mother had laid it all out on the kitchen table.

I stood there for a moment, looking at everything I had carefully hidden beneath my bed, the violation of it just sitting there out in the open washing over me in black waves.

We'd had a fight earlier, our worst ever. I had stormed out—something I never did—and left to meet my best friend at a late-night diner.

"Be home by eleven!" my mom had shouted at me over the bang of the slammed door. It was my curfew, but my parents never bothered enforcing it unless they were angry at me, those rare times when we were in a power struggle.

I walked over to the table. The map was spread open along the table. I reached down to touch it, flinched at the edges. It was too vulnerable, like touching an open wound.

My journals were stacked next to the map.

My mother was sitting in the corner, shrouded in shadow.

"We've talked about this," she said.

"No, *you've* talked about it."

"When were you planning on telling us?"

I shrugged, my hands still running along the familiar creases of the open map. "When there was something to tell."

My mother gestured toward the stack of journals on

the table. Where was my father? "Seems like there is plenty."

I clenched my hands into fits by my side. "Those are private."

"I'm sorry to break your trust, but it's for your—"

"Are you?" I snapped my head up, eyes filled with tears. "*Sorry?*"

"Faye-baby . . . "

"Don't. I'm not your baby. I'm not *anyone's* baby. I'm sixteen." Even as I said the words, they sounded petulant and whiny.

"You'll always be my baby." There was something wild about the way my mother said those words. It reminded me of being six years old, witnessing my sister's birth.

"That's what you don't get," I said. "You won't give me *space*. You're suffocating me. I'm sick of this place."

"This *place* is our home."

"Haven't you ever wondered? About what else there is? Don't you ever feel trapped?"

My mother was silent. "Of course," she finally whispered. "I have *wondered*. We all have. But when you understand how special this place is, what it costs . . . The privilege of safety, such a precious thing—"

"Fuck safety! I am sick of being *safe*. I want to *live*."

"You don't appreciate all your father and I have given."

"You're right. I don't. I never asked for this life."

"You don't understand. What I would give. To protect you. To protect . . . *all* of you."

"I am dying here. On the inside. I have to know what else there is."

"You can't leave," my mother whispered.

"I can't? Or you won't let me?"

My mother smiled, faintly, wistfully. "I know how alluring it is to think of what else might be out there. I understand that pull. That curiosity. I do. But, my Faye-

159

baby, all the world is the same, really—with one key difference. Nowhere is safe like Edgewood. It's—"

"I know," I said. And I did. I had heard it my whole life, had grown up with it engrained in me. "Edgewood is special. *Everyone* knows that."

My mother emerged from the shadows then, into the kitchen light. She traced her fingers along the creases in the map until they met mine. She squeezed my hand with the gentle authority I had grown to trust and love—and to resent.

"What you sacrifice," she whispered, "you gain a thousand-fold. The rewards are so much greater than the—*small*—price you pay in return."

I pulled away from her grasp. *The price you paid.* What she meant was freedom. Everyone in Edgewood was *free* to leave. No one stayed against their will.

But no one ever *actually* left. Not for vacations, for school, for work—not for anything. Fear of what might happen should we venture beyond Edgewood's borders kept everyone in place.

And that wasn't freedom, to me. That was manipulation. The thought of staying there forever, of never taking a risk, never taking a chance—it was stifling. Suffocating.

There's no place like home, they said.

But how do you know that's true, unless you taste the rest of the world?

"I can't stay."

My mother nodded. "It's ultimately your choice, Faye, and I want it to be your own. I trust when the time comes, you'll know what's right."

What she meant was, she wanted me to choose what she wanted. I had never asked to be town steward. It wasn't a role I wanted. I wanted—well, I didn't know what I wanted. Just . . . *more.* And I needed to leave Edgewood to find it.

"Did you really read them all?" The thought stabbed right through my heart, an ache of violation to think of my mother reading all of my raw and vulnerable thoughts.

"Not—*all*," she said, her voice quiet. Then she amended: "Enough."

Those thoughts weren't for her. This was exactly why I needed to get out of this place. We were all over each other here. There wasn't room to breathe. If I stayed, I was going to grow into the mold they'd already made for me. The mold was ill-fitting, and wrong, and I couldn't bear to think what parts of me I would lose if I was forced to fit into it.

"You can't make me stay forever."

"You're right. I can't."

I shrugged. "When I'm eighteen . . . "

"That's still two years away. While you're under our roof, you'll—"

"I'll what, Mom? I can't dream? Are you telling me what I can think now, too? So much for freedom. Yeah. Edgewood. It's so *wonderful*." The word tasted lethal in my mouth, and I spit it at her like a poisoned dart.

"Our family has worked hard," my mother said, like I'd insulted her very being. And in a way, I suppose I had. For her, Edgewood was personal.

"I never *asked* to be in this family."

"No," my mother said, her voice soft and subdued in a way that made me hate her, because it was meant to make me feel sorry for her. "No, Faye-baby, you didn't. But I asked for you. I asked the forest. And I got you—my faery daughter. My light when I needed you most."

And there it was, the guilt, the reminder that, as safe as Edgewood was, it wasn't all the way safe, not if my sister could die.

"Maybe Edgewood isn't what you think it is," I said.

My mother's eyes widened. "Oh, no, that's where you're wrong. Edgewood is exactly what it's meant to be. We've made it this way. We've ensured it."

"I didn't ask for this."

"None of us did. And yet, here we are. What a gift. You'll understand that, one day, I know you will. I believe in you. Edgewood is ours, darling, *ours*. Isn't that wonderful?"

It didn't feel wonderful. It didn't feel like a gift. What I was starting to understand, even then, what I knew in my heart but couldn't articulate or understand was that sometimes, there wasn't much difference between a gift and a curse.

CHAPTER THIRTY-THREE

I'D HAD ENOUGH of Edgewood's containment. What did my mother know of dreams? It was possible to exist outside of our small world. Why did safety matter? Why couldn't I choose for myself?

Choice. My father had always told me that I had a choice. That I was free. I could leave any time I wanted. Well, I *wanted*. And I wasn't going to wait until I turned eighteen.

I brushed at the tears that burned hot trails on my cheeks. Who was my mother to tell me what I could dream, to keep me from tracing the lines on my maps? I was done looking at maps, tired of unfolding and folding, of tucking them underneath my bed and staying in my room, where it was "safe."

I was in the forest, a backpack filled hastily with clothes and granola bars, and I had left the trails, was pushing my way through the overgrown forest brush and shrubs, the tangled vines hanging off trees. Enough, already. Enough. They'd see. She'd see. We were prisoners here. Who needed Edgewood's protection? I didn't. What was the point of being safe if you never got to *live*?

I moved faster, with each step a little more certain. I was really going to do this. I was *doing* it. The closer I got to the border, the more my blood sang.

I slowed when I saw them. The two stone pillars that announced the east end of Edgewood's borders. Slowly,

163

with an attitude akin to reverence, I approached the pillars. The stone was cool and hard beneath my fingertips. Steady, sturdy, strong, secure. I felt them beneath my hands, thought of all the years I'd stood here, looking with longing at the world beyond them but not daring to step even an inch past them. How could I have? I was young, and my ears were full of whispered warnings, of tales of the harm that would befall me if I dared.

All of that would change today. I was brave. I wasn't afraid of *stories*. The world beyond the pillars looked exactly the same as the one in which my feet were currently planted. How bad could it be?

Just past the two markers, I paused with my feet rooted firmly on the earth and stopped.

My shoulders relaxed into the light weight of my backpack.

I was right. Of course, I had been all along. Nothing was different. These were still the same woods, my same beloved forest. I began to walk, soaking each moment in, savoring the taste of my rebellion.

Edgewood wasn't special, as I had always been told. It was powered by belief and superstition and, worst of all, fear.

I jaunted through the forest, hungry, eager, wanting to see the world, no more waiting, no more wondering, no more being afraid.

But I was too fast, too careless.

The ground was uneven, and my ankle twisted violently in a divot.

I lunged forward into the wild underbrush. My arms flailed uselessly, and I hit the ground, felt a searing white hot pain in my shin.

I lay on the ground, not daring to move, my body absorbing the shock of my fall. With some effort, I sat up and pulled my knee into my chest.

I stared at my leg.

The Forest

A sharp, broken branch had been waiting for me at just the right angle, and it had stabbed straight through my pant leg, penetrated the skin of my shin. It was deeply lodged into my skin, anchored into my muscle. Blood trickled down my leg, out through my wound.

When I finally mustered the courage to yank it out, I howled with pain. Blood sputtered from the angry opening. I set the blood-covered branch on the ground, and with shaking hands, lifted my pant leg. I winced as the material grazed my raw wound.

The mangle of flesh and blood and muscle was awe-inspiring. The hole was wide and gaping and red. I turned my leg back and forth, the pain so intense it was almost pleasurable, a new sensation, a novelty. I had never been injured before. I peered into the hole and glimpsed white.

I scooted over to a nearby tree and leaned against it, watched my bleeding wound while I contemplated.

Was this a coincidence? My first time beyond Edgewood's borders and I was badly hurt? *Was* the world beyond my home a hostile place? My wound wept blood. I was starting to feel dizzy and nauseous. The light was turning golden, slanting behind the trees. It was just a matter of time before dark.

The reality of what I was doing hit me, and I was no longer sure that this was how I wanted to go about it. I didn't want to be alone in the dark in these foreign woods, this wild place beyond my home.

Home.

Was it true, then? Was there no place like it?

Suddenly I felt very cold. And afraid. I would leave Edgewood one day. I would. That day just wouldn't be today. The woods echoed with the scurrying of animals, the rustling of leaves. My blood turned cold and I left a trail of it behind me while I limped back toward those two stone pillars. These woods were no place for a wounded creature at night.

I didn't know how I was going to explain this wound to my parents. This wasn't the kind of thing that happened in Edgewood. There were no such things as "accidents." I wouldn't be able to hide an injury this severe, and they would know I'd been beyond the borders.

My blood was fizzing, my skin sizzling like bacon cooking.

And then it started to itch, the fiercest itch I'd ever felt in my life. The blood on my leg pooled upward, drawing itself back into the wound, which smelled like burning, tarring flesh.

Then, from the inside, my wound began to heal.

The burning itch was worse just before the wound healed completely. I shrieked and dropped to my bottom. I squeezed my eyes shut and rocked back and forth, held onto my wounded leg, helpless.

And just as quickly as it had begun, it was over.

The pain, the itch, gone. Just like that.

My shin was smooth and blemish free. I traced my fingers along the place where a gaping wound had been mere moments before. Nothing. Not even a hint of a scar.

It was true, then. Everything I'd been told my whole life. It wasn't just stories. Edgewood *was* protected, and anything could happen in the world beyond its borders.

The thought should have comforted me, but it only made me feel worse. We really did have a choice: safety, or chance. Familiarity, or adventure. But that adventure would come with a price, maybe one I wasn't prepared to pay.

Chapter Thirty-Four

THE HEAT OF Charlie's body was a new sensation against my own. We were in the back seat of his Oldsmobile sedan, parked at the edge of the forest. The windows were cracked but the summer air was humid. I had never felt more alive than I did in that moment, with every nerve lit with the electricity of desire.

What I'd noticed first about Charlie were his lips: round and full and red. That red contrasted with his soft dark scruff, just enough on his face and chin. There was a soft dip at the center of his top lip that made my stomach raw with a new kind of hunger.

I'd had crushes before but Charlie was different. This was urgent, and immediate, from the moment I first saw him.

His smell filled the back of the car: deodorant and soap and something else, the earthy spice of cedar. My hands roved beneath his t-shirt, his skin moist and hot with sweat and desire. Things that should've been gross just weren't in these moments: that's what I was discovering about intimacy.

We hadn't had sex yet.

We'd fooled around plenty, played at the edges.

I hadn't thought much about sex before—I'd actively avoided it, avoided boys—but that was all Faye, B.C.: *Before Charlie*.

Charlie arrived in town, and my resolve crumbled.

It worried me, how willing I was to forget everything in favor of him. How eager I was to discard my dreams and replace them with new ones, ones that involved Charlie and stupid, simple things like sharing a home and having a family. Making babies that would look like some astonishing combination of both of us.

I was afraid of who I was becoming. Afraid of betraying who I was when I was young.

The maps were still stashed beneath my bed, but I hadn't looked at them in the months since Charlie had arrived.

Guilt washed over me, when I was alone. When the smell of Charlie wasn't there to intoxicate and distract me, I was still aware of my plans. Determined to see them through. I couldn't be the girl who threw away everything she'd ever dreamed of for some boy. That story was so cliché—it couldn't possibly be mine. I wouldn't let it be mine. I would enjoy Charlie for the summer, and then in the fall, I would leave Edgewood. Just as I had always planned.

It was easy to think all this, when I was alone, when Charlie wasn't touching me in places no one but I had ever touched.

And Charlie was here. Charlie's earthy, cedar smell filling up the car, filling up my heart. Charlie taking off my shirt, unbuttoning my pants.

Dreams were one thing, but Charlie was real. Charlie was now. What else could I find out there that would make me feel as good as Charlie's tongue on the soft skin inside my thighs? What else could there possibly be that would make me feel this damn alive?

Charlie pulled off my underwear, and we were both naked, together. There was a new smell, an animal one. It didn't feel weird, to let him see and smell me. It made me real.

Charlie sat back in the seat then. "This okay?"

I nodded. "Yes, but," I sat up and pressed my hand to Charlie's chest, "you have one, right?"

But Charlie was already fumbling with his jeans that had fallen to the floor of the back seat. "Yeah."

I grinned at him. "Prepared?"

Even in the dark, I saw the sudden pink flush on his cheeks. "It wasn't—I just figured, you know, we've been messing around, and you know, just in case, we should be safe—"

I leaned into him, pressed my finger to his lips. My nipples grazed his chest. "I'm teasing. I'm glad. I wouldn't want to risk—" but I didn't say it. Instead, I shrugged. "*You* know. Not on our first time."

Charlie fumbled nervously with the condom, slid it onto himself. I watched. The condom was important. I wasn't ready for more, not yet.

I lay back on the seat, and Charlie leaned over me. His breath was hot in my face and it smelled animal and it smelled good. He pressed himself between my legs. I opened, a soft pop of release when he pushed his full self inside.

I gasped, a low moan.

Charlie stopped. "Still okay?"

"Yeah," I whispered, pulling his face into mine. "Still okay."

When I gave Charlie my virginity, I gave him all the secret parts of me. Charlie punctured my dreams. They shifted and changed, morphing in color and shape and texture and taste and even origin. They became anchored by a new tether. Charlie. Me. Edgewood.

Who we were, who we would become *together*.

The maps *stayed* folded beneath my bed, after that.

I didn't think of them for a long time.

Chapter Thirty-Five

JONAS WAS ONLY three weeks old. It was the end of a day when he'd been "cluster-feeding"—meaning, he wanted to nurse every hour or sometimes, even as much as every thirty minutes.

I was spent: emotionally, physically, spiritually.

I had just finished nursing Jonas for what felt like the thousandth time that day. I'd handed him over to Charlie, hoping for a few minutes of reprieve from Jonas' relentless *needing*. I leaned back on our couch and closed my eyes, hoping to capture a few minutes of elusive sleep.

I hadn't had a full night's sleep since before Jonas was born. My body felt foreign. My stomach sagged with loose, jellied skin, the empty sac that once protected Jonas. The raw pain of my stitched-up vaginal tear meant I had to use pillows to pad my backside. My breasts were swollen and heavy with milk. Jonas wasn't the only newborn: I, too, was a newly born mother, my leaking body sore and molten and strong from my metamorphosis.

My mother was with us, as she had been every day since Jonas was born. She was in the kitchen, preparing a warm, comforting supper. I didn't know if I could have survived the challenge of those early days without her constant help, her keen ability to know what was needed, and when, and her ability to deftly and simply help, without being an intrusion.

No sooner had I leaned back in the chair than Jonas

began to cry. Those mewling, newborn cries clawed at my insides, tugged at all of my mother bear instincts. Something warm leaked from between my legs. My eyes opened. The corner of Jonas' mouth bumped Charlie's shoulder, triggering his rooting reflex and signaling his hunger.

"Again?" I groaned. "Already?"

Charlie shrugged, helpless, and patted Jonas' tiny back.

I reached for Jonas, arms heavy. My body felt, not only foreign, but *not mine*.

My body hadn't belonged to me since before the pregnancy.

All I wanted was an hour. Just one. An hour to be alone. To not be needed. An hour to care about my *own* needs. An hour to reconnect with this new me. She wasn't familiar and I hadn't had a chance to get to know her. It was like living in a stranger's body.

I helped Jonas attach to my breast. He had a strong, healthy, open-mouthed latch, and even so, after nursing so frequently, my nipples were tender and swollen and raw.

These were supposed to be the happiest days of my life, and I was filled with sorrow.

It was as though a part of myself had died, *forever*, and I hadn't had a chance to mourn her.

I belonged to Jonas, now. I was his nurturer, his food source. I didn't feel like a whole person. I no longer had space for dreams.

Charlie was by the front door, strapping on his running shoes.

The space between my eyebrows hardened, creased.

"What?" Charlie said.

"Running?"

"I need to feel like myself."

"Like yourself."

"Since he was born, I've only got to run a handful of times. I'm a little stir crazy."

"You're stir crazy. *You*."

"Are you saying I don't do anything? I can't nurse him. I'm just sitting here. I need to blow off some steam."

"Go ahead. Go blow off steam."

"Now I feel guilty."

"Whatever." My throat felt swollen, thick with envy, with grief for those lost pieces of myself, and I blinked back tears. "Just go."

He went. Out to run in the woods, free to spend a few moments being just himself and no one else, with no one connected to him, no one needing him like Jonas needed me. Free to breathe in the fresh pine smell of the trees and the damp smell of fresh earth.

Free.

Would I ever feel free again? *Could* I ever feel free again? I felt horrible for having those thoughts, for resenting my sweet baby. How could I love someone with such unbearable ferocity, yet also despise them in such dark moments as this?

A deep, dark depression yawned open, and I tumbled headfirst into it.

Only three weeks in, and I was already a horrible mother.

What if something happened to him? Wasn't that the punishment I deserved for having such selfish, evil thoughts?

I couldn't help it. Guttural sobs tore savagely at my already-ravaged insides. My mouth hung open, a gaping, dark cavern trickling out spit. My cheeks were wet with tears, front lip glazed with snot.

Then I felt my mother's arms around me, slow at first, almost timid. Then warmer, stronger, fiercer.

"I know, I *know*," she whispered.

Jonas still suckled at my breast, a ravenous, wanting thing—relentless in his hunger, his need.

"It's—so much," I choked, between sobs.

"You went so long just you," my mother said into my hair. "Only needing to worry about you. Able to do what you want, whenever."

"And Charlie."

"It's different for fathers. They won't understand, not in the same way."

"I'm not—he's not—He helps me so much. I'm just so—I'm so—*jealous*."

"I know, baby." My mother's voice was low and gentle. It soothed me, all the way down to my bones, only the way the voice you've heard since before you were born could.

"I don't even like running," I said. "It's just—"

"I know, my baby. I know."

I looked down at Jonas, then. "And I feel so guilty." This, barely a whisper. "He can't help it. He just needs me."

My mother smoothed my hair back. "Welcome to motherhood," she said with a rueful smile. "A constant vacillation between selfishness and selflessness. You'd do anything for them, and at times you'd throw them to the wolves for a moment of peace."

"Am I a terrible mother? Is it awful to feel this way?"

"Oh, Faye-baby, no. How you're feeling is completely normal."

I laughed, unexpectedly. Then I was quiet, thoughtful, the tears wet stains on my cheeks. Jonas wasn't nursing anymore, but flat on his back in my lap, his dark eyes reflecting light in a way that made them look like they contained universes. I bent down to kiss his soft cheek and breathe in his sweet, milky smell. "It's overwhelming," I said, and inhaled him, smiled down at his wide, bewildered newborn face. My voice lowered, a sound meant just for him. "But I could never leave you to the wolves."

"It's all worth it," my mother said. "Even the sacrifice."

PART THREE

SACRIFICE

CHAPTER THIRTY-SIX

LIGHT SLICES INTO my skull.

The trees above me spin sickeningly. I sit up but the nausea is too much and I vomit. Did I throw up before, or was that a dream?

I remember a black cloak, and I cast my gaze around the small clearing where I was sleeping.

Sleeping.

How long was I asleep for? And why was I sleeping?

My stomach churns with anxiety, with questions.

Where am I? *When* am I?

The horrible, painfully bright light that filters in through the trees is garish and orange. Orange.

It is late afternoon, approaching sunset. We need to get moving.

I reach for Jonas. He isn't here.

Jonas.

I press my hands to my temples, will the sharp ringing to stop, the terrible pain to cease.

Breathe.

It's fine. Jonas is okay. He probably just crawled away again. Oh, god, how long was I out?

There are so many evils in these woods, so many dangers. We aren't in Edgewood anymore. We aren't protected. Bad things can happen here. Tragedies both small and great. We are at the mercy of fate in these woods. Of nature.

Wild animals. The search party. A black cloak.

My head spins with confusion and panic, the blood in my veins slow and syrupy. My body is heavy with fatigue. I can't see straight, can't think. The light hurts my skull.

I sit up but move impossibly slow. I can't muster a sense of urgency. *Move*. Find Jonas. Where is he? Where is my baby?

The panic renders me shaky and slow, but I whirl around, searching.

My movements are too sudden for my sludgy brain to keep up and I fall over, throw up again.

I cry while I puke, despair surging, and I think, absurdly, of the lost Rowan necklace. It had felt like an omen, a loss of protection. I am a woman who grew up with magic, with talismans, with mystical protections. Is it such a stretch to think the necklace was protecting us in some significant way, and now that it's gone, so is our luck?

I weep—deep, noiseless. I am failing my son. I have failed. I haven't saved Jonas. I've as good as killed him.

I am a terrible mother.

I stand again, despite the pounding in my head, despite the dizziness, the disorientation. I can't tell which way is which, and there are no clues to Jonas' whereabouts. I clench my fists so hard my fingernails dig into my calloused hands.

"Jonas!" I scream into the woods. The exertion makes me dizzier and I wobble, grip a tree for support. "Jonas!" I scream again. I don't care if they hear me. I need to find my baby.

"Jonas!"

My throat is ragged from screaming, from crying, from puking.

Then I hear it.

A voice, nearby, saying, "She's awake."

Chapter Thirty-Seven

CHARLIE

    He grabs my arm, gently, but even still, I yank it away. He holds both hands up, even though *I* am the one who is meant to yield.

Nothing feels real, and everything feels too real. The juxtaposition is nauseating. I could still be sleeping, still in a cluster of leaves and pine needles, still following that black cloak, still in the river, dead.

Anything is possible in this moment. Everything, and nothing.

It is over.

Charlie starts to walk, and I follow. What choice do I have?

"Jonas." It's the only thing I can bring myself to say, the only thing I still have energy for.

Charlie doesn't turn around, trusts I am still following. He knows I will. He knows I am too weak to do anything else. Knows the fight has left me.

"He's fine," Charlie says. "Safe."

"Safe," I mutter, the word meaningless to me now. And yet: Jonas is still alive. My baby is still here. There is still a chance that I might save him.

But the sun is setting on the Equinox, and I know that whatever time we have left is running out.

Still.

If I get to hold him—smell his sweet and sour soft milk

smell, press my face into the soft skin of his neck, kiss his soft pink cheeks—just one more time, maybe I can breathe enough of him in to carry his memory with me forever.

It's all I can do now.

Commit him to memory. Bear witness to his existence.

My mother waits for us in the clearing, holding Jonas. There is a bandage on her head—and I sense the memory of when I hit her, another time, another place, so far away.

The flush of relief I feel at seeing Jonas, alive and pink and wiggling and wrapped in a warm blanket in my mother's arms is quickly followed by a nauseating swell of fear.

Townspeople encircle the clearing, large wooden clubs in hand. They aren't taking any chances this time. I swallow.

Dad stands next to my mother, staring at the ground, twisting his large, freckled hands in front of him. I glare at him.

"See?" Charlie says. "Jonas is safe."

"Safe." I say that word, quietly, softly, almost to myself. It's lost all texture and meaning.

Because in my mother's arms, Jonas looks anything but safe.

My hands clench into fists again, my fingernails digging half-moons into my palms. I focus on the sharp, shrill pain of it, ripe and raw, focus on that sensation rather than the ringing in my ears, the throbbing in my temples, the nausea that coils and unfurls itself in my bowels, the sharp assault of light in my skull.

I am not doing well.

Every part of me aches.

My heart worst of all.

I can't bear it, can't think of it, I lean over to throw up again but I just stand there, bent over and gagging. There is nothing left. I am empty, hollow. I can feel myself surrendering, giving up.

The Forest

I just want to hold my baby.

"Please," I whisper.

My mother takes one step back, away from me.

"Please. I won't run."

My mother shakes her head, and I can see her grip tighten. The gesture fills me with anger. My fists moisten with the slick, wet heat of my blood. She has no right. No *right*. Jonas doesn't belong to her.

"He's my son," I hiss through gritted teeth. I want to bare them at her, snarl like a mother wolf protecting her pup.

"You aren't well, Faye-baby," she says. I flinch at the nickname, an inappropriate violation of intimacy. I stiffen, purposely and obviously. I want her to see my disgust, want her to know I am out of grace. "You hit your head, in the river. A concussion is likely."

"I'm fine," I say, even as the world spins around me, threatens to tip over.

"Are you?" My mother raises a brow, presses her cheek to Jonas', a sight that makes my heart ache. I need to be close to him. "No nausea?"

She says this having just witnessed my attempt to vomit. She pauses and her silence is pregnant with accusation. I lift my chin.

She continues, "No sensitivity to light? No headache, sleepiness? *Confusion*?" This last she emphasizes.

I shake my head, stubborn, resolute. It doesn't matter that what she says is true, that in all likelihood I do have a concussion. That's a red herring, something to distract me from what's really important.

"Give me my son." I pronounce each word with careful precision.

My mother clicks her tongue. She manages to make it a sad sound, a sorry sound, a mourning sound. "Oh, Faye-baby. You're tired. This has all been so disorienting, I'm sure."

"*Disorienting*?" I say, disbelief dripping from my tongue. I want to scream at her, You're goddamn right! But I don't say anything else, can't bring myself to speak another word. I struggle to keep the wobble out of my stance, push back hard against the dizziness. I point at my father. "He helped me," I say, and my father looks up at me, quickly, a flash of agony before staring again at the forest floor. "Yesterday. He saw us and he helped us get away."

My mother turns to him. "Is this true?"

My father ignores her, the forest floor suddenly much more interesting.

"You know it's wrong." I spit the words right at him, like poison darts. "Yet you allow it to continue. You won't fight for us. And you know what? That makes you worst of all." This time I physically spit on the ground. I want him to feel my disgust, my loathing.

My mother turns away from him.

"It doesn't matter," she says. "We're here now."

Yes. Yes, we are here. Nowhere left to go, nowhere to run. The bright orange fades to a deep burnt red. The light still hurts my head, but it isn't as bright now, isn't as invasive. The sun is setting on the Equinox, and we are out of time.

My mother lifts a walkie-talkie to her lips. We have cell phones, but my parents have always liked to do things the old-fashioned way. The thought strikes me suddenly as terribly sad. It's their firm commitment to tradition—to the way *things have always been done*—that is at the root of all this heartache.

She pushes the black button on top of the radio and it chirps. "We're coming."

The walkie-talkie beeps again, followed by a crackle of static on the speaker. "Ready for ya."

Sheriff Wilson.

I follow my mother. What other choice do I have? She has my son.

The worst part of all of this is how content Jonas is in my mother's arms. How much he trusts her. He can't help himself; he doesn't know any better.

At that thought, my mouth moistens with hot saliva and I think I might be sick again.

Jonas is so innocent, so sweet and trusting. This world hasn't tarnished him yet, hasn't taught him that people can lie, that things aren't always what they appear to be. And it seems so unfair, that he will be the one to suffer.

We reach the road in an astonishingly short amount of time.

When we emerge from the forest, I stop at the treeline. I clench my hands into fists again, dig deeper into those fresh cuts.

We'd been so close. *So close*.

A caravan of cars awaits us and the rest of the search party. Sheriff Wilson has blockaded the road with squad cars, their blue and red lights flashing. I smirk. He finally has a purpose, after all.

My body is weary.

My cheeks are wet with tears.

Jonas starts to cry, and instinctively, I move toward my mother. Charlie steps forward, grabs my arm. I yank it away.

"It's okay," my mother says, eying Charlie.

"He's hungry," I say, realizing just now how full my breasts are, how hard with milk. "He needs to nurse."

My mother hesitates, then nods. "All right." She points to her dark blue Forester. "Sit in the back. We'll all be just outside."

I know what she means by that. It's a warning, not to run. Not to try anything foolish.

But all of this feels foolish, every last thing. My farce of a marriage, my joke of a family. Things that mere days ago had meant the world to me—had been my *everything*—but which had proven to be a façade. It had never been real. None of it.

I was the one who'd been duped. Fooled.

I pull Jonas into my arms, blanket and all, and he is soft and squirming and wonderful. I press my face into the soft crook of his neck and inhale, breathe him in.

Jonas is real.

My love for him is real.

His need for me—to nurture and protect him—is real.

I don't know what is worse: that most everything in my life has been a lie, or that they want to take away the one thing that's actually true.

I climb into the back seat of my parents' Subaru with Jonas, sink into the worn material. Jonas is fussy—hungry— and he is close to me now, can sense what is coming.

I still feel dizzy, my head throbs, but those sensations are overshadowed by the physical rush of relief my body feels at having Jonas back in my arms.

The ache of being separated from him is physical, an actual feeling of absence, of something missing. We are a dyad, a nursing mother and son. He may not live inside my body anymore, but our bodies still depend on each other for nourishment. For life.

I hold him close, listen to his gulping, swallowing sounds.

I drink them in as though they're our last moments, because maybe they are.

Jonas' golden eyelashes, fluttery and feathery-soft against his pink-white cheeks. The little tuft of hair at the tops of his ears, that make him look elfin. I touch the palm of his hand and he wraps his tiny chubby fingers around it. Tiny, slightly rounded fingernails. Soft indentations at the knuckles. Unbearably adorable, perfect miniature versions of adult hands.

I memorize his scent: a salty, sweet, slightly sour milk smell that is particular only to him—like it's something I can store up inside myself, bottle, save for later so I can take it out from time to time, and remember.

184

I kiss the top of his head. "I love you," I whisper. "I am still here. *Always*."

My mother raps on the window. "It's getting late."

I nod. "We're finishing up," I say, though it's not really true, though I know that we could stay here like this forever, intertwined, each drawing comfort from the other.

I am grateful to have had these moments.

A shock of pain stabs through my chest when I unlatch Jonas, when I acknowledge that this moment is over.

There is a car seat next to me—a small detail I am unbearably grateful for, though at this point any pretense of protection seems cruel, a mockery.

I strap Jonas in, anyway. He protests at first, but I pluck a pacifier from the car seat's cup holder and hand it to him. "There you go." Jonas settles and I strap him in, make sure the straps are tight and secure. Then I sit back, next to him, buckle my own seatbelt.

I place my finger into Jonas' hand again, and he grips it, as he always does. A reflex. An instinct.

I look out the car window, meet my mother's eye. Hold it.

Finally, I nod. A concession. *We're ready*, even though we never will be.

She breaks my gaze—*she* is the one to look away, I held her eyes, made her look at me, made her *see* into me, bear witness to what she was doing. She climbs into the driver's seat, and my father slides in, wordlessly, next to her. Charlie gets in the car, too, sits on the other side of Jonas. Charlie reaches for Jonas' hair, and my hand darts out for his, a snake uncoiled, and stops him.

I meet Charlie's eyes across the car seat, and his eyes are begging, pleading with me to understand.

But I will not understand.

I do not.

His are the eyes of a stranger.

I turn my attention back to Jonas. If these are my last

moments with him, I want to really be here with him. To remember every little thing. To appreciate it.

I think of those early days, when I was so sleep deprived and anxious and elated, and a sour rush of bitterness fills me.

I wished those days away, and now they are gone.

I can never get them back.

Those days, those moments, are gone, and now we are here.

I would give anything to go back, to do it all over again, to slow down, to laugh through the exhaustion, to know that it doesn't last forever, it can't last forever.

And oh, what a tragedy that is.

Nothing lasts forever.

My mother pulls out onto the road. The sky is grey and purple and darkening, dusk. The headlights illuminate our way back to Edgewood.

I smear my tears away so I can see Jonas, so I can be here with him.

And we go on, driving in the wrong direction, back to the place that I once called home. There's nowhere like it.

Nowhere in the world.

Aren't we the lucky ones?

CHAPTER THIRTY-EIGHT

AT MY PARENTS' house the air sizzles with nervous energy. Everyone cleans the forest dirt and grime off themselves.

Even I'm allowed to wash, though I take no joy in it. Blossom waits outside the bathroom door, has been instructed by my mother to alert them if I try anything.

My mother gave me clothes to wear—black jeans, a black shirt with long sleeves, but I leave them folded on top of the toilet.

I won't wear some uniform she's prepared for me. I am here because I have to be. I'm a prisoner. But I won't play their games, won't cooperate beyond what's necessary for survival.

I run the bathroom faucet on hot, as hot as it will go. I splash that scalding water over my face and I can almost feel my pores open. I didn't want to clean up but the nausea has worsened and the artificial lights in my parents' home are even worse than the garish sunset light had been.

The hot water is a relief for my throbbing head, my disjointed brain. I wish I could think clearly, wish I could remember everything that happened. My memories of this afternoon, from the moment I emerged from the river with Jonas to the moment I stepped inside my parents' house, are like disconnected snapshots. How did we get from there to here?

It seems so hopeless, so futile, that we'd have made it so far only to be right back where we started.

All that wasted energy.

I failed Jonas.

My face crumples and I press it into the hand towel I retrieved from its perch above the sink. It is blue and the fibers are soft and worn, a relic from my childhood, a childhood whose nostalgia is lies, all lies.

I toss the towel into a corner like it's a poisonous snake. I don't want to be in this house, around these people, reminded of a childhood so golden and happy and miraculous it feels like an insult held up against the harsh truth of what these people want me to do.

I look in the mirror, though it makes me dizzy to focus on my reflection. I squint. The longer I stare, the more disconnected from myself I feel. It's like I'm looking at a stranger, and I wait for the woman in the mirror to move without my prompting. Her face is pitying and I despise her pity.

It makes me want to break the glass.

The door bangs and I jump.

The sound sends my head pulsing again, throbbing. God, it hurts.

"What?" My voice is more of a snarl than I'd intended, but I don't care.

Even as I think it, I know it isn't true.

I still love them, every single one. It makes this so much worse, so much more difficult to swallow.

If I could just hate them, I could shake all of this off. But we are all tangled together. Me, my mother, my father, Blossom, Arrow, Charlie.

Jonas.

At least, *I* am tangled with them.

But even worse than that is I want to wake up, for this to all have been a long, horrible dream. I could wake up in a hot sweat, Charlie in bed next to me, rubbing my shoulders, drawing me into his chest, the cedar smell of him bringing me back down to earth.

I could cry and I could tell him about this horrible dream, this absurd nightmare.

And you were there, and you, and you, and you.

But this isn't a children's story. Dorothy gets to wake up and realize *there's no place like home*, but not me.

The banging on the door comes again, louder and more insistent, and this time, it's accompanied by my sister's voice, an octave higher than it should be. "Faye?" A pause. The next time she speaks, her voice is lower, softer. "Are you okay?"

I open the door, just as Blossom was about the knock again. We stand there like that, eye to eye, face to face, sister to sister.

I don't bother to hide what I think of all of this, what I think of my family. I'm not trying to protect them. Only Jonas.

I let my disgust shine through, my anger.

"Oh, Faye. I'm so sorry."

"Are you?" It's my question to everyone lately.

"You know I am," she says, flustered, reaching for me. But I flinch away. "I tried to stop them. I held them off for as long as I could."

Anger wells up within me, but I know it's not at her. "We can't let this happen."

Blossom twists her fingers together. "I know."

"My family wants to murder my son." I pronounce each word slowly, let them take hard and cold shape in the air. "What am I supposed to do?"

She throws her arms above her head, then buries her face into her hands. "I don't know. Mom is—she's—"

"She's fucking terrifying. It's like she's a stranger."

"I'll help in any way I can. I'll—"

"It's time," my mother is saying. Her voice rings through the entire house like a bell. Or an alarm.

LISA QUIGLEY

I shove past Blossom, roughly, even though none of this is her fault, and the jarring motion sets my head spinning all over again.

My physical condition is frustrating. I struggle to think clearly, to process what I see and hear. In the living room, my mother has dressed Jonas in a black—nightgown? dress?—and placed him in the wicker Moses basket that she bought for us when he was born.

Jonas used to sleep in that basket in the early days. I would carry him with me from room to room, listen to his soft snores.

I realize now that my mother always had plans for this basket.

My gut twists. I think of Jonas sleeping in that basket, all those hours, so tiny and new. Like he was sleeping in his own grave.

Everyone is dressed in black.

I'm still wearing the same dirty clothes I've been wearing for days.

My mother finishes tucking Jonas into the Moses basket, wrapping him in black blankets.

It's funny—I had never really thought about that name for it before. Moses. Now the story cuts into my heart. The thought of a mother's love, so fierce, so primal, that she would do anything for her child: even send him down the river in a basket.

Because staying meant certain death.

The river was—well, it was probable death. Not certain. Sending her baby down the river in a basket, though it was risky and he would probably die, was his only hope.

I think of that mother, terrified, desperate and willing to do anything to protect her son. I think of how her heart must have broken, shattered, to watch her baby disappear on the surface of the water. How she prayed. How she hoped.

I can't stop the tears.

190

The Forest

My mother's crying, too.

An anger so hot, so fiery, consumes me and I almost lash out. I want to hit her again, crack her skull. I bite my lip until I taste the tang of blood.

"Faye, I know this is hard, but please understand. The balance *must* be restored. Waiting like you did, it weakened things."

"It isn't your *place*," I say. "It isn't your decision."

"And you think it's *yours*?" my mother says. "This is so much bigger than just you. Or just Jonas."

Just Jonas. I shake my head, because Jonas is *everything*.

My mother turns to the others. "We're ready."

But I'm not through with her. I grab her by the sleeve, and she turns back harshly. The look in her eyes is shocking, wild, raw.

I let her go. I will not find an ally in her, or anyone here. Just my mess of a family. Something inside me breaks.

Only the immediate family can be present for the ceremony. It's a private thing. Not for the rest of the town to witness.

Isn't that charming? They can all eat their dinners in their cozy homes, sleep in their warm beds, bask in the safety bought by our sacrifice.

The thought makes me want to puke.

This town is poisoned. Tainted. I want nothing to do with it. I want to burn it. Leave, and never look back.

My fingernails reopen wounds on my palms.

My father stares at the floor—always at the floor. Look up. *Look at me*. At us. We are right here.

Your daughter.

Your grandson.

You can stop this.

But he doesn't, and I don't say any of those things.

My mother scoops up the basket, leading the way out

the door, and we follow. Our matriarch, our fearless leader. She leads, we follow. It is how it has always been.

We take the back way, cutting through yards and dipping through dead end streets.

We finally stop at the edge of the forest on the back side of the town. The same place Charlie and I had come to park when we were young and stupid and hungry for each other. Where I had given my virginity to him.

The irony is a punch in the gut.

Of course, *of course* we would come to the place where it all started.

Hundreds of unlit black candles await at the edge of the forest, spread out in a large circle. My mother stops the group when we reach the center of those candles, and faces us. "Now the ceremony can begin."

CHAPTER THIRTY-NINE

WE STAND IN the center of the circle, and my mother nods at Blossom, but she shakes her head. Her arms are crossed over her body, her jaw set. No. My mother sighs and turns to Arrow, whose eyes are lit with triumphant fire.

He pulls something long from the pocket on his sweater. A kitchen lighter. He begins lighting each of the black candles, moving with such slow, purposeful reverence it makes my nausea flare.

My mother approaches the forest with the basket. It is already dark, with only the faintest ambient light leftover from sunset on the horizon behind us. The forest itself is darker, the spaces between the trees steeped in shadows.

This is agony of the worst kind.

"Wait!" I shriek. "Won't you let me kiss him goodbye?"

My mother stops, her back to me. She looks over her shoulder, meets my gaze with piercing, sharp eyes. I used to think that sharpness reflected her precision, her carefulness, but now I see it so clearly I don't know how I missed it before. All my life.

My mother is insane.

Her eyebrows gather together, and her face floods with misguided concern. She shakes her head. "It will be easier this way. Pull the band-aid."

The band-aid.

As though losing Jonas is a scrape of the knee, a blip, a minor wound that will scab over and heal.

The image is so absurd, so incongruous against the terrible stabbing in my chest, a gaping wound that will never reach the bottom, will never close. A black abyss of grief that goes on for eternity.

There will be no remedy strong enough to repair such devastation.

Not even time.

Arrow finishes lighting the candles and resumes his place next to our father. My father's jaw is set but his cheeks glisten with tears. His betrayal hurts most of all.

This strange circle of candlelight at the edge of the forest is a perversion of comfort, just like all the rest of the safe things in my life.

My mother places the basket on the ground, so the opening is facing the forest. I can't even see his face. She bends to place a kiss on his forehead, an abomination.

I take off toward the edge of the forest, toward the basket, but Charlie is quick on my heels, quick to wrap me in his arms—arms I once loved, arms I *do* still love, the worst thing of all—and it is terrible, oh so terrible to be so betrayed by the person—the people—I trusted most in the world.

Charlie keeps his arms around me, an unwanted embrace, and I collapse to my knees.

"Please." It's a whisper at first, but the next time I open my mouth it's a scream. "Please!"

The sound is shocking, even to my own ears.

It's a primal sound, a sound only a mother could make, a sound ripped from my womb, the place that has bled and blossomed and bloomed with life, that nurtured and protected and grew my son. The place that is empty now.

My breath comes in ragged, aching gasps.

I feel like I'm dying and wish that I was.

"Please god no!" My screams cut through the night.

The Forest

"Take me! Take me instead. Please let me have my baby. My baby!"

The sounds that escape my mouth become guttural noises that transcend language.

A language only mothers can understand.

The language of grief.

Of loss.

Strands of saliva stretch from lips, snot slides from my nose into my open mouth. I howl.

I lost.

This is it.

I failed my son.

My mother leaves Jonas at the edge of the forest, walks back to us. She stops where I kneel and helps Charlie lift me to my feet.

The fight has drained out of me. The thought that I am giving up makes me sick, but I don't have the strength to try.

But there is nothing left but the thick black mourning that has filled me up like a liquid, a tar—and it makes me slow and tired and compliant.

Here I am, the girl I've always been, the girl who gives in, who gives up.

I'm no better than the rest of them.

I should keep fighting. I should do something.

But I'm at a loss. I am defeated.

It's over.

I let them guide me back to the center of the circle.

My mother directs us all to face the forest edge.

"Kneel."

The group kneels.

I stay standing, in my non-black clothes, my chin lifted in the air, my jaw set, one final act of defiance.

My mother places her terrible firm hands on my shoulders. She presses her lips to my ears. Her breath is hot and humid, revolting.

"It's for the common good," she whispers. "It's bigger than you, or Jonas, or any one person. It's for our town, and everyone in it. Remember that. Carry it with you in the terrible moments to come. I won't lie to you. I won't say it's easy. But remembering, well, it will ease the burden of my grief."

She pushes down, hard.

I resist it at first, but she's hurting me, and I ache enough already. Finally, I acquiesce.

The burden of my grief.

As though this grief is something I will carry, not something that is a part of me, eating away until there is only empty space.

I kneel with the rest of them.

A final betrayal against my son.

This time, it's me who does it.

My eyes fill with tears and my head hangs. I sob, so deep and all-encompassing that it is soundless, from the empty place where my baby once lived. The only time he was ever safe.

And yet, I realize now, clearly, he never was.

Our safety is—has always been—an illusion.

It's not something you can ever guarantee, and it's foolish to try to manipulate that.

No matter how hard you try to keep bad things from happening, the darkness always has a way of creeping in. And maybe we think we've found a way around that in Edgewood—a loophole—but there's always a price to pay.

And we're paying it.

All of us.

Not just me.

Paying for it with our souls, with our humanity. I am not blameless in this. I should have known—my mother has been trying to tell me all these years. It's always been there, between the lines.

The Forest

I have always known that Edgewood's safety wasn't free, that it was bought and paid for with sacrifice.

I have always known that darkness lurked.

I have always known that when something is too good to be true, then it isn't.

I am complicit.

We all are.

I will not abandon my baby in these final moments. I will not look away. I will not be too cowardly to watch.

I am his mother, and he deserves that at the very least.

I will myself to look up, to keep my eyes on Jonas.

And two figures in black cloaks emerge from the forest.

CHAPTER FORTY

THEIR FACES ARE shadowed by hoods.

The one in front is very old, and in charge. I understand these things, somehow, although I don't know this, couldn't articulate if I tried. The answers come from some place deep within my womb, the place of intuition and understanding.

The second figure has something wrapped around her waist, something familiar, but I can't make out what it is in this dark. Somehow I understand these figures to be women.

That isn't quite right.

They are both women and not women. In this world, but not of it. They are something *else*. Something other.

Human, but also not *quite*.

They move toward the basket, maintaining their strange formation, their slow, rustling movements.

The wind shifts, and I smell it.

The stench of forest rot: decaying leaves and pine needles and moss.

The first one, the leader, is dizzying to look at head-on. Her face shimmers and shifts like a mirage. She is a very old woman, with a strange long nose and wild white hair; at the same time, her skin is comprised of leaves and moss and earth.

All of this is ridiculous, impossible, because I can't see either of their faces in the dark.

The Forest

I remind myself I am injured; I can't trust what I see, or what I *think* I see.

Jonas' cry pierces the black night, and my heart.

"Oh, baby," I murmur and try to calm myself for his sake. I call to him, hoping that my voice won't carry any of my agony to him on the night breeze. That he will only feel my love, my apology. "It's okay, baby. It's gonna be okay."

All parents lie to their children.

The old woman—*is she an old woman?*—kneels before my Jonas.

My body tenses.

Charlie and my mother each take an arm, anticipate my urge to run.

Never have I felt so helpless.

The cloaked figure reaches into the basket, retrieves my Jonas.

"Please," I cry into the night. My heart prays for mercy, even though I don't believe in God. "*Please.* Take me instead. I'll give you anything—anything you want. Just please. Spare my baby. Please spare him. Please. I'll go. *Take me.* Take me instead."

The woman stands. Her arms are wrapped around Jonas, carefully, almost—lovingly? *Reverently.*

Jonas stops crying.

He is looking up into that face hidden by shadows.

What does he see, I wonder?

Can babies see the truth? Is their perception unfiltered by bias?

The two move closer, walking in unison, still in their strangely angled formation.

They stop at the edge of the candlelit circle.

The forest stink is unbearable.

"What is this?" I hear my mother say these words, but my brain can't filter it through all the noise in my head, the buzzing, the static, can't understand what they mean. "This isn't—"

She stops talking when the duo crosses the candle barrier. My mother cries out, but the noise seems to come from some other place, some other universe.

I know who they are. They were with me in the forest, were with me in the tunnel. One of them helped me out of the river.

It's absurd, but it's also true.

They are not the enemy.

CHAPTER FORTY-ONE

EVERY TIME I try to look at the old woman, I can't bring her into focus. Just when I think I have a grip on her appearance, she shifts, changes, morphs. I second-guess myself because of my head injury. Things cannot be as strange as they seem, and yet, despite my reeling, despite my nausea, despite my throbbing head: all of this feels very, very real.

Again, my mother says, "This isn't how it goes."

But all my focus is on the old woman. Search her weathered-skin-not-skin-moss face. I reach for Jonas, but her grip is resolute.

"What is this?" My mother's panic strangles her.

My father grabs her arm, shushes her.

Finally, the old woman speaks.

Or—I think she does.

It isn't a language that I know.

It sounds like leaves rustling; like branches snapping; like river water rushing. It sounds like all of these at once, and none of these.

I also understand her.

The sensation is disorienting, overwhelming, like I've been split into two people, like I'm standing beside another version of myself from another universe, and we're both experiencing this moment differently, but because we are the same person, we can feel what the other person is feeling.

Everything goes still.

A calmness hits me.

These creatures—women?—are not the enemy.

What she tells me—tells all of us—is this:

Your mother is right. Wind through trees. *This isn't how it goes.* Water over smooth rocks.

The tongue with which she speaks is crude and ancient. Terrifying and beautiful.

I listen, mesmerized, my veins coursing with the deep magic of it all, the wonder. Jonas nuzzles against her chest. A thing he never does with strangers.

Not the enemy.

Still, she does have my son.

"Please," I say. "Let me have him."

I risk a glance at the rest of the group, and I can tell by the bewitched looks on all of their faces that they, too, can understand her strange language.

It's in all of us. The thought is just there—my thought; this is different from the woman-creature speaking—and even though I have no idea what it means, I feel in my core that it is true. *We're born with it.*

Your mother is right, the hag says again.

I think that word—*hag*—with something akin to reverence.

This isn't the way it goes. But that burden is on her; not on us.

"I don't understand," my mother says. "I did what was required. I brought the sacrifice."

But the hag waves her off like a pesky fly.

You know the rules.

"I do," my mother says, panic edging her words in neon. She can't hide. Not anymore. Things are not going according to plan, and my mother can't ignore it. "That's why we are here. We have brought you the child of the new stewards. We demand that you honor the deal."

But you have not honored our deal. This, a snarl: the

sharp, warning sound that a wolf makes deep in the back of its throat.

My mother's arms flail wildly as my father holds her waist. "What do you mean?" my mother spits. "We've brought the child. It's the equinox. It's all in line with the arrangement."

Almost, the old woman says. *Almost, but not quite. There is one very important part of the deal that you're forgetting.*

Who *is* this woman-creature? *What* is she?

She smells like the forest floor after a good rain, like wet earth and fallen leaves and damp moss.

The sacrifice must be a willing one.

My mother has lost complete control of her voice. It is shrill and wild and uncontained.

The mother must not be forced.

My mother yanks on my shoulder. "Faye, do something. You heard her. Stop being foolish. This is for *everyone*. It's so much bigger than you and this one baby. Don't you *get* that?"

I whirl on her, so close we are nose to nose. I don't back down. In this moment, I have renewed strength: I exhale the fire of my breath into her face.

"This *one* baby? That's all Jonas is to you? He is *everything* to me. The one baby. The *only* baby. I would do anything to save him."

"Clearly," my mother says.

"Yes," I say, indignant. "Yes, clearly! What kind of mother would I be to do anything different?"

"You know nothing about any of this. Nothing."

My father pulls my mother away from me. "Lois." His voice is low but firm. "Enough."

"You," my mother says. "This is *your* fault. *You* did this. You filled her head with nonsense. Fed her dreams so she could never be satiated by Edgewood."

"Maybe Edgewood did that," my father says. "You ever think of that? You ever think this place isn't so perfect?"

LISA QUIGLEY

But already my mother is shaking her head. "Never. *Never*. How can you say that? Think it? This is an *oasis*. A haven. Our *safe* place."

The word that has lost all meaning.

It sounds so sad—so empty and hollow and meaningless—when she says it.

Another word for *trapped*.

Another word for *can't leave*.

I reach for Jonas. "May I?" The words are barely a whisper.

For one brief, horrible moment I fear we will freeze like this, a terrible tableau of this never-ending moment.

But then the old woman's arms are outstretched, and Jonas is in my arms, and I am crying, and my tears wet his cheeks. I kiss him, breathe in his sour-sweet milk smell, that salty Jonas smell and this, *this* is heaven.

He nuzzles into me and I feel dizzy with gratitude, so overwhelmed I fear I might faint.

My mother's voice: "This isn't how it's done! Think of the town. Think of everyone. This is for them. It has always been for *them*."

"Has it?" I snap, turning to my mother once again, cradling Jonas into my chest. I am speaking to my mother but I am also fully present with him, aware of the soft feel of him, the wonderful smell. Knowing I will never take another moment with him for granted. "Or is it for you? So you don't have to look at what you've done? So you don't have to realize that you had a choice? You could have stopped this. You could have saved Autumn. That's what this is really all about, isn't it?"

"You don't know what you're talking about," my mother says. "You don't—"

Enough.

The creature's voice is loud and quiet at the same time, and it vibrates in the air, it carries the weight of authority,

204

the electricity of a summer thunderstorm. Each of us go still and silent when she speaks.

Then, for the first time, the other woman—the younger woman—breaks the strange formation that they have so far kept with impeccable precision.

And now this other cloaked figure—a young woman that I somehow understand is a young woman despite having never seen her face—stands in front of me.

She wears the same black cloak as the old woman—crude and without flair—but now that she is close, I can see what it is around her waist.

It is a thin leather belt, and what hangs from it are three chicken carcasses in varying degrees of decay.

All of the chickens are missing their legs.

I search for her features in the shadowed face of the cloaked figure.

She lowers her black hood. It falls without theatrics.

The young woman's face doesn't morph like the old hag's. It is solidly human, and uncannily familiar.

Suddenly my whole family is murmuring, buzzing, alive with wonder and curiosity and terror.

Because we know these eyes. *I* know these eyes, this face.

Her eyes are the same pale grey as our father's; her skin is the same pale moonlight as our mother's.

CHAPTER FORTY-TWO

"**A**UTUMN," I WHISPER. Her hair color is a faded, mousy brown: not at all the brilliant, maple leaf red that I'd always imagined.

She cocks her head quizzically, doesn't speak, her expression a mixture of mirth and confusion.

Of course, she wouldn't know her name. Of course, it *isn't* her name. It's just what we have selfishly called her, in order to preserve the memory of someone we had no right to remember.

Because she hadn't died.

Because she had been abandoned.

The cruelty of it makes the saliva sour in my mouth, the acrid taste of shame. That we had the audacity to live such a sheltered, perfect, privileged life, while she was out here in the forest, discarded, unused, unloved. I think again of my childhood, of my father building me ships in the trees, of my daydreams about maps and faraway places, the way the sunlight slanted through the forest trees.

All of it was a lie.

I hold Jonas even closer to me. He is not a commodity. He is not a bargaining chip.

I stare at this young woman who is and who is *not* Autumn; who is both my sister and *not* my sister.

"I'm sorry," I say.

The young woman who was once Autumn examines me with a quizzical-yet-warm expression. She reaches to touch my cheek; then her fingers gently graze Jonas' puff of hair. She bends, then pauses, eyebrows raised quizzically.

I nod.

Jonas snuggles against my chest, and the woman who was once my sister presses her lips to the top of his head and I could live in this perfect moment forever.

But of course, there are others in this circle, and my mother has finally come into herself. She vibrates at a manic frequency.

"Autumn?" My mother—and it is true: she is my mother; Arrow's mother; Blossom's mother; *not* Autumn's mother; she can't claim that right—leaps forward, ripping free of my father's weakened grasp. "Is it you? Is it really *you*? It can't be, after all these years, after all this time? You're here? You're—*here*?"

Then my mother takes Autumn's face into her hands and this feral young woman who was once my sister recoils, her face darkened with alarm—no, not alarm: *fury*—at the intrusion of my mother's touch.

And of course. Why wouldn't she react this way? She is a wild woman, a feral woman, a creature of the forest.

I think of how my mother used to call me her forest creature and I see now how very wrong she was.

A forest creature does not sit safely within the boundaries that someone else created for her. A forest creature does not build a careful life.

A forest creature *roams*. A forest creature *hunts*. A forest creature explores and survives and takes *risks*.

This woman?

This woman who snarls at the touch of a human?

This woman who has learned not to trust?

This woman who lives in the wild world and survives, and thrives?

This is a forest creature.

I am not worthy.

I never was.

I am Faye, but she is *Autumn*.

I look at my mother, really look at her. In several of the books I've read in our modest town library, I've often come across the description "they looked as though they've seen a ghost." It's a cliché, and maybe a little silly. What does a person look like when they've seen a ghost?

But in this moment my mother beholds the young woman who was once my sister with an expression that is a terrifying mixture of both horror and wonder and I understand the expression.

It's the only way I could ever describe how my mother looks right now, because for her, Autumn *is* a ghost.

All these years, my parents have believed her to be dead. When they abandoned her to the whims of the forest, as far as they knew, they *were* sentencing her to death.

We don't always have to face the sins of our past with such blatant immediacy.

My mother's hands are now meekly by her side, balled into fists, digging half-moons into her palms, just like I do.

"You're alive, oh my baby, you're *alive*."

Her face is twisted in anguish: the kind that I recognize because I have felt it myself. Because it's the kind of anguish that comes from deep within a woman's womb. That same womb that grew and nurtured babies, from which sprouts an unbearable instinct to protect. In spite of myself, I am filled with pity. It is true that she brought this on herself, but in this moment, she is just a mother.

My mother. Ours.

I want to wrap my arms around her, to comfort her. I have an unbearable urge to tell her that it will be okay, that she's forgiven.

The urge sickens me. I stuff it down.

It will *never* be okay.

What my mother did—and what she tried to force me to do—is unforgivable. It doesn't matter that she's sorry now that Autumn is in front of her. Autumn is no longer a story she can twist and manipulate to mean something different, something that makes sense, something that serves her purposes. Autumn is a living, breathing human.

Her cold grey eyes hold no love, because why should they? What does she owe my mother but indifference at best, and hatred at worst?

My heart swells with unwanted love for the damaged woman in front of me, the woman whose womb carried me, protected me, nourished me. The woman whose body sustained me with milk for my first year of life. The woman who taught me, comforted me, chastised me, held me, brainwashed me.

I love her because I cannot help but love her.

I love her because she is my mother.

The love hurts the most, because it's a part of me, woven into the fabric of my skin and heart.

It hurts because I don't know if my mother is possible of this same kind of helpless love for me. I don't know that she has ever seen me as her daughter, as an individual. She has never celebrated my differences. She has only worked very hard to mold me into the person she wanted me to be.

I hold Jonas to me closely, promise that I will hold him tightly, but not *too* tightly. My cheeks are wet with tears and I press them to Jonas'.

"I see you," I whisper, low enough that no one else can hear. This moment is for me and him.

My father takes my mother's hand and pulls her away from Autumn, away from us, toward the edge of the circle.

"No!" my mother shrieks. "It isn't right! I am her mother. Her *mother*. I want to hold her."

The audacity of her words strikes me like ice water. Who is she to speak of what is right and what isn't? Who is she to use that word, to call herself *mother*?

My tears turn hot and angry. So many emotions

warring for dominance within me and I feel suddenly so weary, so dizzy and hungry and tired. I want to rest. I want to take my baby home and sleep.

My sister reaches inside her cloak and when her hand reemerges, she is holding something.

The Rowan bead necklace.

She extends her hands to me, the necklace entangled in her fingers. An offering.

I look from her to the necklace and I am struck with recognition. I don't reach for it. Instead, I say, "You." My voice is filled with wonder. "It was you, at the river. You tried to save us."

My sister keeps her hand outstretched, doesn't reply. I don't even know if she can speak, if she understands my words. But then she nods. A shy, sheepish nod and suddenly she doesn't seem so feral. She is just a girl, and this hand outstretched is an offering of love.

My heart swells.

I shake my head. "You keep it. The necklace. It's yours. It was always yours. I was keeping it safe for you."

For one precarious moment, Autumn keeps her hand outstretched. Then clutches the necklace to her chest. She understands my meaning. My intent.

I smile.

Autumn slips the necklace around her neck. Then she reaches back into her cloak, and turns toward the old woman, her face a question that I can't decipher.

The old woman nods. *It's time,* the hag says, and her voice is like fallen leaves, like the creaking trunks of ancient trees.

Autumn's hand emerges from the cloak, and I gasp. The knife glints in the candlelight. I half-turn away, an instinctual, protective movement because Jonas is still in my arms.

Autumn offers me the knife, hilt first.

The old hag is speaking again.

There are other ways to satisfy the arrangement, she says. Wind moving through trees. Howls hooting in the middle of the night. *A blood sacrifice is desirable.*

"Blood?" My throat has gone dry; my insides are like icy river water.

You are the mother, she says. The scream of cicadas. *It is your choice.*

"Mine?"

I take the knife from her hand and lower it to my side, search the faces of my family. My ears thrum; my head throbs.

"Is this—required?"

Continued protection requires exchange, the old woman says.

"But I—they're my family," I say.

They were willing, the old woman says. The shriek of a harpy.

The hag is neutral—neither good nor evil. She doesn't operate on human rules. She is guided by forces much more ancient than that.

My family regards me now with open terror on their faces, yes, and something more—something more foul.

Shame.

None of them are blameless.

And they know it.

Each of them stands there, rooted to the spot, knowing that I could choose any one of them—all of them, even—as an offering, and I would be justified in my vengeance.

But I am not innocent, either. I have benefitted from their shame.

My hand hangs limply by my side, weighed down by the knife.

There is Charlie, his dark hair curled around his face, dampened with sweat. Those thick lashes that looked like soft feathers in the right light. The full lips I used to kiss.

There is Arrow, who waded thigh-deep into the river

to help me catch crawdads every summer. Arrow who never combs his hair, and who always seems too long for his clothes and his bed. Arrow, who is a quick runner, a quicker thinker.

There is Blossom, whose birth I witnessed. Blossom who never understood my love of the outdoors, my obsession with boats and treehouses. Blossom who played with dolls while I played with dirt. Blossom who supported me without question.

There is my father. The man who helped me build my treeship, who acquired my maps, taught me to dream. The man who pretended not to notice when I snuck books from the shelves in his office. The man who never said so outright, but taught me all the same that there was more to the world than Edgewood. The man who didn't stand up for me and my son, who helped us get away in the woods.

And there is my mother, her face looking so drawn and worn and tired, so lost in a way that is incongruous with everything I have ever known her to be. My mother who has never shown a sign of doubt. My mother who wanted me to give my son, just as she once gave her daughter. Whose head is wrapped in a bandage covering my violence against her. My mother, caught up in a cycle more ancient and unknowable than even she can fully understand, who wanted to drag me into the same cycle without question, without the threat of challenge or rebellion.

I have known and loved and cherished my family, and all of the anger I should feel toward each of them melts and sizzles down to nothing, fat dripping from a grill. With the anger melted away, all I feel is love, raw and bare. It burns like an open wound exposed to air.

I drop the knife, hear the hungry slice of the blade plunging into the soft earth at my feet.

Autumn stands before me, my oldest sister—if I even have the right to call her that, after all these years, after basking in the spoils bought with her life. I shake my head, hold Jonas a little closer. He squirms and fusses against my grip, against the cold, against the discomfort of this unusual night. My poor baby. I kiss the top of his head. I just want to retreat with him to a warm, safe space. To nurse him and hold him close and breathe the smell of him in and let him drift to sleep, safe in the security of knowing I will protect him fiercely against the unfairness of the world, in the comfort of knowing he is loved.

"I won't do it," I say, my jaw setting with resolution. "Whatever the consequences."

Very well, replies the voice like autumn leaves under rodent feet.

"Wait!"

My mother's voice is dangerous in its desperation, and I barely manage a half-turn before she is kneeling at my side.

The knife is in her hand.

And then it happens so fast that we barely have time to register, to react with more than the collective intake of our breaths, in unison, a chorus in this dark, candlelit evening.

Her blood looks black in the flickering light, a thick dark line against the pale skin of her strong, veined wrist.

My mother extends her arm toward the two cloaked figures, her head bowed in supplication.

"Please." Her voice is a whisper, a prayer, and the blood spills out of her, so rich, so thick, so shiny and dark and slick on the grass.

I'm sorry, the old hag says, and her voice is like a mournful wind.

And my father has come to his senses, removes his shirt, lunges for my mother who thrashes against him while he ties his shirt around her arm, creates a tourniquet.

"No!" My mother's scream comes from a place I recognize, from her womb, from the place only a woman can access.

I realize then, with the quiet horror that comes only with the most unbearable of truths, that my mother believes without question, that she sees the town as her true child, the one she is meant to protect with as much devotion as I feel it in my veins to protect Jonas.

She carries the duty of a mother, just not to us.

Not to the children she bore from her womb.

My father staunches the bleeding, and my mother stops struggling against him, sobbing into his chest.

"But what will we do?" She cries. She *mourns*. For to her, this is the greatest of losses.

And I feel sympathy for her. Not empathy—never that—but on some level, I can understand that she has just lost the most cherished piece of her existence, what she has believed to be her destiny, her purpose. She has lost the very thing that held her together, that kept her sane. The thing she would give her life for, has been willing to exchange her children and grandchildren for.

All that sacrifice, all that belief, all that unquestioning devotion.

And for what?

My heart squeezes with pity because I see the moment my mother breaks beyond repair, and I know she will never be the same woman again.

The cloaked figures are retreating into the forest, but the old hag's voice floats to us like leaves on the winds.

You will live. You will love. You will hurt. You will delight. You will die.

"But what will we tell them?" my mother screams as they retreat.

Before they disappear into the woods, their home, before they enter the forest: *The truth. Tell them they are human.*

Wind extinguishes the candle flames, and my mother's screams gouge the blackness of the night.

Chapter Forty-Three

I**T'S THE FIRST** day that feels truly autumn all season: the air is crisp, edged with the faintest suggestion of winter. Early in the morning, when I'd stepped into the backyard to empty some of the things I would not be taking with me into the trash can, my breath had frosted white clouds in the golden early morning sunlight.

My things are packed. I am only taking the most basic of essentials. My clothes. Favorite books. My maps.

Jonas will need more than me, of course. Still, I focus on essentials and a few favorite toys and books. Whatever we take with us needs to fit into the car.

I've made my decision, but I'm still human. I'm not cut off from emotion. In fact, I'm drowning in it.

There is a vinyl decal forest on the nursery walls, with creatures—birds, deer, raccoons, owls, foxes—that peek out from behind them. Carefully arranged stuffed animals, a quilt that matches the colors in the nursery perfectly: greens, reds, oranges, browns.

In the hopeful days before Jonas was born, Charlie and I spent many late nights in this room, dreaming about Jonas' arrival, anticipating all the ways our lives were about to change. We coped with this nervous energy by preparing this room. A room that Jonas didn't even use in his first few months of life.

It had been important to me to pay tribute to the forest in Jonas' nursery. Those days of preparation feel like an entire lifetime ago. We were so naïve, so ignorant of the truth. We were so willing to believe in the stability of the cocoon we had constructed that we hadn't been willing to see how it had also trapped and limited us.

I think on some level I always felt that, always knew.

It was just easier to ignore the awful, gaping truths that whispered from the bottom of things.

Of course, that is impossible now.

Edgewood is tainted forever.

I touch the soft, plush fox on Jonas' changing table. I still love the forest, even though it isn't exactly as I had imagined it to be in my youth. I don't blame the forest for any of this. The forest is just doing what nature does to survive.

We are human, and we should have known better than to strike a deal with forces we don't understand, with consequences we couldn't quite comprehend.

Dorothy woke up from her dream to realize that there's no place like home, and of course, for her, it's true. Dorothy is a story. Fiction.

This is reality, and everything that had come before: that was the dream. When we thought we were untouchable, invincible. When we were so foolish to believe we had gamed the system.

And what kind of story teaches you to stay put? That it's safer where you are?

The room darkens. I don't have to look up to know that Charlie stands in the doorway.

It's been like this ever since we returned to our house. Charlie hasn't said much, but he has lurked around our edges, watching, always in our orbit. I can feel the anxiety radiating from him, darkening the room with more than just his shadow.

"What?" I finally say, without looking up from my task of packing.

"You don't have to do this."

"I don't have a choice."

"We always have choices."

"Is that right?" An orange stuffed fox on the dresser catches a ray of sunlight through the open window, and I pick it up.

"Faye." Charlie steps into the room, violating our unspoken agreement of keeping space between us. "I fucked up. I know I did. I—"

"It's too late. Where were you when it mattered?"

"I was scared."

"You were scared. *You.*"

"I don't want to lose you."

"Oh, Charlie." I sigh and return to what little there is left to pack. "It's far too late for that."

"I love you," Charlie says, and his voice drops to barely a whisper. "I love you both."

"I know," I say, and I swallow, tears threatening for the first time since we've returned from our ordeal. "I love you, too."

It isn't simple. It is true that everything is irrevocably changed, and that we can't go back. It is also true that everything is more complex than hard black and white lines. Just because I can't stay here, can't be with Charlie, can't reconcile the harsh truth of what he was willing to do with the possibility of any kind of future together, doesn't mean that I have stopped loving him, or that I ever will.

Charlie breaches the distance, cuts through the space between us. His face is wild with agony, with regret. He wraps his arms around me and I smell his soapy cedar scent, feel the hot warm strength of his embrace. He buries his face in my neck and I feel the wet of his tears against my skin.

I soften into his embrace, a gesture of regret, of empathy, but not of yielding. We need this moment for closure, but I am resolved in my decision. Already the smell of him has the quality of nostalgia, a thing I will catch on a random breeze in the future and remember with a pang of longing. Charlie is my past, but not my future.

"Please don't go."

"I have to. *We* have to."

"Then let me go with you. I can make it up to you."

"No. You can't."

I kiss his cheek. A farewell, not a promise.

***

My family gathers in our driveway after I get the car loaded. Charlie stands apart from them, his eyes red-rimmed, his bottom lip quivering. He hasn't stopped looking at Jonas.

My mother's head and wrist are wrapped in bandages, her face forlorn. She stands next to my father, who isn't touching her as he usually is. His weathered, work-worn hands are clasped tightly together in front of himself, but he stands tall.

"You'll write?" he says, close to tears.

"You'll visit?"

He pulls me into himself. "Go, baby girl. See the world. Have your adventures. Teach Jonas to take risks. I'm so sorry."

My heart squeezes in my chest and I pull back. "You're a *good* dad. You know that? You are."

"I lost my way. I know that now."

Blossom stands slightly behind them, her face determined. "I'm coming with you."

I shake my head. "I don't think so."

"It's not your call," Blossoms says, tossing her blonde curls. "I can ride with you, or I can follow you. Either way, I'm going."

"But your stuff?"

She grins. "Bags already packed." And she runs inside.

Arrow stands in solidarity with my mother, whose expression is vacant.

I shake Arrow's hand. "Take care of her," I whisper.

"You'll make a great town steward. It was always meant to be you."

Arrow shrugs. "I'm sorry," he says. "I am. I just—really wanted to matter."

"You always have," I say. "To me."

He shrugs. "It should have been enough."

"Yeah, well."

"Will you come back? I don't know if I can make it without my big sis."

I scan the shapes that make up my family, the edges and curves I have known my whole life. What will a life without them look like? To never spend another whole Saturday baking with my mother, or talking about books with my father. To never argue with Arrow. To never spend another lazy Sunday at the Edgewood river with Blossom. To never make love to Charlie.

"I can't promise anything."

It's the truth.

"It won't be the same here." My mother's voice is flat. No pretense or elaboration, as is her way.

"It won't," I say.

She shrinks into herself, disappears into a place where I cannot follow. Where none of us can.

Each of them hugs me, then kisses Jonas. It should be awkward but it isn't. They've betrayed me, yes, but they're my family. They're all I have ever known. Their bodies smell like home. A pang of longing cuts through me. I swallow, fighting back tears.

Charlie lingers at Jonas.

"Don't take him," he murmurs, lips pressed against Jonas' soft golden-brown curls at the base of his neck.

"I can't leave him," I say.

"Then stay." His voice even lower now; one last try.

I pull Charlie close, press my lips to his ear. "You know I can't. And you know why."

We stay like that for one long, cedar-scented moment,

our three bodies intertwined, our lips pressed to each other.

Then we untangle. We separate.

My father looks younger somehow. He's the only one in the group without an air of defeat. He seems more alive, buoyant.

He pulls me to him, presses his lips first to the top of my head and then to the top of Jonas'. "If you need anything, call. Write. I'll help you anyway I can. You were right, you know, this whole time. You were right. I should have done more. And sooner. I wasn't strong. But you. You were strong for all of us. You're a wonderful mother. An incredible daughter. You're going to make it, out there. You'll do great things."

"I'm hoping to just survive."

"Sometimes, baby girl, that's enough."

I swallow the sudden obstruction in my throat. "I love you."

"You have the maps?"

I smile, because this is our code, and beneath these words, my father is saying everything. "Yeah. I have them."

"Good. I know there's high tech stuff now, but a good map will never steer you wrong. Remember what I taught you."

"How could I forget?"

He pulls me close again, squeezes a little harder this time. Then he lets me go.

Blossom bangs out of the front door with her bag, hurls it into my car. She says her goodbyes.

I buckle Jonas into his car seat, make sure he's secure. It's the kind of precaution we have always taken in Edgewood—better not to tempt fate—but it never felt truly necessary. But when I finish tightening the harness, it feels symbolic in a way that turns my spine to ice. He looks so vulnerable, so unprotected despite all the straps. It doesn't seem like nearly enough protection in a world with unlimited potential for both ecstasy and heartache.

THE FOREST

I stoop down to place a kiss on his forehead, then close the door.

I climb into the driver's seat, close the door. I buckle my seatbelt. These small, habitual precautions feel so weighted with potential, with significance. What will it be like, out there in a world without boundaries, without edges or rules? What will it be like to wake up each day, and know that it could possibly be my last?

The questions swell in my chest, make it difficult to breathe, but I gulp air through my open mouth anyway. I squeeze my eyes shut, then open them. I start the car.

I'm doing this.

Blossom reaches for my hand on the steering wheel and squeezes.

We're doing this.

I don't really know what I'm doing. I don't know where we'll live, how we'll make it. I don't know how I'll manage to support Jonas and raise him at the same time—all I know is that I can't stay here, and I have to try. I will find a way. I will.

I shift the car into reverse, back slowly out of the driveway. I pause at the end, observe my family in their disordered line.

And still, after everything—despite everything—my heart swells with love. I smile. *I'm okay. I'll be okay.* I wave at them. *Goodbye.*

I am careful to look both ways a number of times before finally pulling out. Each decision carries with it the weight of consequence, and I won't take that responsibility lightly.

The roads wind their way toward the edge of town, and I follow them. I am careful to pay attention, noticing each house in this neighborhood I have known and loved. My body is alive with ache, with nostalgia, the sensation of loss. This is the place where I grew up, and whatever else I may feel about it, I did love it.

221

I love it still. Maybe I always will.

We drive past the town square, past the shops and the park at the center of town.

I make a final right turn onto the main road, the one that leads to elsewhere.

Something moves at the forest line.

A young woman with light brown hair.

"Faye," Blossom says.

I pull over to the shoulder.

Autumn no longer wears the black cloak. Instead she's dressed in rags, her hair a tangled mess around her shoulders.

I roll down the window. "Hey."

Autumn doesn't respond.

"Do you want to come with us?"

She studies us: from me to Blossom, to Jonas in the car seat, then back to me. I don't know if she understands a word.

I meet her eyes again, more earnestly this time. "Come," I say. "Please."

She opens the door and climbs into the back seat, where she appears so foreign and wild. I grin, and she closes the door.

I hit the gas.

I don't know what the future holds. All I do know is that at this moment, the road stretches long and wide and open, full of promise, and terror. Leaving won't right the wrongs of the past, but it's a start.

I don't know where we're going, but we're going there together.

I take a deep and shaky breath.

And we drive.

ACKNOWLEDGEMENTS

In most fairy tales and folklore, magic has a cost. For me, creativity is magic, and this story cost me my engagement ring.

When we first moved to New Jersey, I discovered a trail in the woods by my in-law's house. I walked this trail nearly every day. I was a new mom, living in a new state, missing my friends, my community, the comfort and familiarity of California. The trail was my saving grace. It was my refuge, my daily connection to nature. Some days I walked alone. Others, with my son strapped to my chest.

One evening, I was getting ready for bed when I realized I had lost my engagement ring. I looked out the window at the woods. In the same moment I realized I had left my ring in my pocket, I received the story of *The Forest* in its entirety.

I don't really know where I lost the ring. It could have been anywhere else I'd been that day. But I like to think it's still somewhere in those woods.

Most of this book was drafted in my head and/or problem-solved on that trail. So: thank you to the trees, the river, the blue jays, the robins, the chipmunks, the squirrels, the deer, the rabbits, the mosquitos, the cicadas, the insects, the soil, the rocks, and the rains.

Thank you also to the Lenni-Lenape tribe, on whose unceded land this story was conceived, written, and edited.

Special thanks to the University of California Riverside, Palm Desert Low Residency MFA Program faculty: Tod Goldberg, Stephen Graham Jones, Mark Haskell Smith, David Ulin, and Mary Waters. Each of you met me at crucial points of my writing journey. I do not believe I'd be where I am today if you all hadn't modeled the myriad possibilities so beautifully.

Thank you to Joe and Barbara Quigley for giving our family a home and letting us live with you way longer than we probably should have. I wrote the first several drafts of this book under your roof in Cranford. Also to the entire Quigley clan for cheering me on in each iteration of my writing journey.

To my parents, John and Lori Morford, who encouraged my love of reading and never censored the books I read. You never discouraged my writing dream, never made me feel like it was silly or impossible or delusional or out of reach. That is rare and I am so so so grateful!

Thank you to Mackenzie Kiera, for being my lifeline across the airwaves. My creative partner in crime, one of my very best friends. You've seen me through it all—the writing frustration, new motherhood, podcasting, the everyday terrors of balancing career and family and passion. I truly do not know where I would be without your endless encouragement, real talk, commiseration, and patience (oh, the patience!)

Thank you to Megan Eccles and Leah Livingston for reading an early draft of this book and believing in it so hard—as well as providing valuable feedback. Also to Eli Ryder and Kathryn McGee, who (in addition to Mackenzie and Megan) comprise the most uplifting, supportive writing group there is.

Kat Howard provided early editorial feedback on this story; without her keen insight, this book wouldn't be what it is.

Endless gratitude to Bob Pastorella, Michael David Wilson, Hailey Piper, Laurel Hightower, Eddie Generous, Tracy Robinson, Shane Douglas Keene, Becky Spratford, Sadie Hartmann, Gwendolyn Kiste, Paul Tremblay, Brian Keene, Josh Malerman, Bracken MacLeod, and the incredible horror writers community for being such a safe space to land.

And of course, thank you to Max Booth III and Lori Michelle at Perpetual Motion Machine Publishing for giving this story a home.

To my best friends Sara Martinez, Ty Hansen, Leah Livingston, Mackenzie Kiera, Danielle Palmese, and Angel Barnes. Late night conversation, too much wine, poolside shenanigans, urgent phone calls—we've been through it all. At various points in my life each one of you has been a lifeline. You've all believed in me even from my earliest days of posting cheesy blogs to blogger.com. You believed in me even when my belief in myself faltered. I treasure each of you. Thank you.

To my husband, Chris Quigley. You don't miss a beat. You understand that I have big dreams and aspirations and put up with my weird podcasting requests (like, please stay in the back room and don't make any noise or you'll mess up the sound quality.) You understand that my head is often in the clouds, and that when I'm walking silently, I'm probably working out a story problem or plotting my next move. You give me the space and time I need to be alone, to write, to dream. You put up with my unusual questions, like, "Do you think it would be possible to walk in a river with a baby on your chest, and for how long?" You are my fiercest advocate and supporter and you're the best dad to our kids. Without your grounding, I'd likely float off into space and never return. You remind me that life is happening here, now—and we're supposed to be having fun. Thank you. I love you.

And finally, to Fallon Joseph and Frances Mercury. You two taught me that a mother's love is the fiercest, most wild thing there is. There is no limit to what I would do for you. You remind me to laugh, to play, to embrace childlike wonder. I would run into every dark forest for you both. My love for you is the lantern that lights my way, till my breath runs out. And probably long, long after.

About the Author

Lisa Quigley is a horror author and pagan witch. She holds an MFA in Creative Writing from the University of California, Riverside's low-residency MFA program in Palm Desert. Her work has appeared in such places as *Unnerving Magazine, Journal of Alta California*, and *Automata Review*. She is the co-host of the award-winning horror fiction podcast Ladies of the Fright. *Hell's Bells* (2020) and *Camp Neverland* (2021) from Unnerving are her novellas. *The Forest* is her debut novel. Lisa lives in New Jersey with one handsome devil and two wild monsters. Find her at www.lisaquigley.net.

IF YOU ENJOYED THE FOREST,
DONT MISS THESE OTHER
TITLES FROM
PERPETUAL MOTION
MACHINE . . .

THE WRTHING SKIES
BY BETTY ROCKSTEADY

ISBN: 978-1-943720-32-3

$12.95

THE SKY IS HUNGRY

Glowing lights and figures in tattered robes force Sarah from her apartment. Outside, phosphorescent creatures infiltrate her every orifice. They want to know everything, especially the things she would rather forget.

Featuring 20 black and white illustrations.

WE NEED TO DO SOMETHING
BY MAX BOOTH III
ISBN: 978-1-943720-45-3
$12.95

A family on the verge of self-destruction finds themselves isolated in their bathroom during a tornado warning.

"Don't look now but Max Booth III is one of the best in horror, and he's only getting started." –Josh Malerman, author of BIRD BOX and MALORIE

Now a major motion picture!

ANTIOCH
BY JESSICA LEONARD
ISBN: 978-1-943720-49-1
$16.95

Antioch used to be a quiet small town where nothing bad ever happened. Now six women have been savagely murdered. The media dubs the killer "Vlad the Impaler" due to the gruesome crime scenes of his victims. Clues are drying up fast and the hunt for the monster responsible is hitting a dead end.

After picking up a late-night transmission on her short-wave radio, a local bookseller named Bess becomes convinced a seventh victim has already been abducted. Bess is used to spending her nights alone reading about Amelia Earhart conspiracy theories, and now a new mystery has fallen in her lap: one she might actually be able to solve.

Assuming she doesn't also wind up abducted.

The Perpetual Motion Machine Catalog

Antioch | Jessica Leonard | Novel

Baby Powder and Other Terrifying Substances | John C. Foster
Story Collection

Bone Saw | Patrick Lacey | Novel

Born in Blood Vols. 1 & 2 | George Daniel Lea | Story Collections

Crabtown, USA:Essays & Observations | Rafael Alvarez | Essays

Dead Men | John Foster | Novel

The Detained | Kristopher Triana | Novella

Eight Eyes that See You Die | W.P. Johnson | Story Collection

The Flying None | Cody Goodfellow | Novella

The Girl in the Video | Michael David Wilson | Novella

Gods on the Lam | Christopher David Rosales | Novel

The Green Kangaroos | Jessica McHugh | Novel

Invasion of the Weirdos | Andrew Hilbert | Novel

Jurassichrist | Michael Allen Rose | Novella

Last Dance in Phoenix | Kurt Reichenbaugh | Novel

Like Jagged Teeth | Betty Rocksteady | Novella

Live On No Evil | Jeremiah Israel | Novel

Lost Films | Various Authors | Anthology

Lost Signals | Various Authors | Anthology

Mojo Rising | Bob Pastorella | Novella

Night Roads | John Foster | Novel

The Nightly Disease | Max Booth III | Novel

Quizzleboon | John Oliver Hodges | Novel

The Ruin Season | Kristopher Triana | Novel

Scanlines | Todd Keisling | Novella

She Was Found in a Guitar Case | David James Keaton | Novel

Standalone | Paul Michael Anderson | Novella

Stealing Propeller Hats from the Dead | David James Keaton | Story Collection

Tales from the Holy Land | Rafael Alvarez | Story Collection

Tales from the Crust | Various Authors | Anthology

The Train Derails in Boston | Jessica McHugh | Novel

Touch the Night | Max Booth III | Novel

We Need to Do Something | Max Booth III | Novella

The Writhing Skies | Betty Rocksteady | Novella

Patreon:
www.patreon.com/pmmpublishing

Website:
www.PerpetualPublishing.com

Facebook:
www.facebook.com/PerpetualPublishing

Twitter:
@PMMPublishing

Newsletter:
www.PMMPNews.com

Email Us:
Contact@PerpetualPublishing.com